Illegitimate Grace   i

Constance Santego

Illegitimate Grace

Dr. Constance Santego brings history to life through the eyes of her great, great… grandaunt in this compelling narrative. Constance resides in beautiful British Columbia, Canada, where she shares a fulfilling life with her husband.

www.constancesantego.ca

Published by
  Editor & Interior Layout: Dr. Constance Santego
  Book Layout: ©2017 BookDesignTemplates.com
  Soft Cover ISBN: 978-1-990062-51-3
  eBook ISBN: 978-1-990062-52-0

Created and published in Canada. Printed and bound in the United States of America
Ordering Information: csantego@gmail.com

ALSO BY DR. CONSTANCE SANTEGO

NOVELS

Okanagan Trilogy:
Beneath the Vineyards
Under the Okanagan Sun
Guardian of the Lake

The Nine Spiritual Gifts Series:
Journey of a Soul – (Vol 1 Michael)
Language of a Soul – (Vol 2 Gabriel)
Prophecy of a Soul – (Vol 3 Bath Kol)
Healing of a Soul – (Vol 4 Raphael)
Miracles of a Soul – (Vol 5 Hamied)
Knowledge of a Soul – (Vol 6 Raziel)
Wisdom of a Soul – (Vol 7 Uriel)
Faith of a Soul – (Vol 8 Pistis Sophia)

NONFICTION
The Intuitive Life, The Gift Of Prophecy, Third Edition
Fairy Tales, Dreams And Reality… Where Are You On Your Path? Second Edition
Your Persona… The Mask You Wear
Angelic Lifestyle, a Vibrant Lifestyle
Angelic Lifestyle 42-Day Energy Cleanse
Archangel Michael's Soul Retrieval Guide
Tesla And The Future Of Energy Medicine
Beyond Tesla: *Advancing The Science Of Energy Healing*
Tesla's Code: *Mastering Energy, Frequency, And Creative Power*
Scaling Beyond 6 Figures: *Strategies for Health & Wellness Professionals*
Beyond the Mind: *Harnessing the Power of Astral Projection for Creative Awakening*
Bend, Don't Break: *Finding Your Way Back to Abundance*
Ring Therapy: *A Guide to Healing and Balance*

Ring Therapy Pocket Guide
Floraopathy™: *The Art and Science of Vibrational Healing
with Essential Oils*

SECRETS OF A HEALER, SERIES:
Magic Of Aromatherapy (Vol I)
Magic Of Reflexology (Vol II)
Magic Of The Gifts (Vol III)
Magic Of Muscle Testing (Vol IV)
Magic Of Iridology (Vol V)
Magic Of Massage (Vol VI)
Magic Of Hypnotherapy (Vol VII)
Magic Of Reiki (Vol VIII)
Magic Of Advanced Aromatherapy (Vol IX)
Magic Of Esthetics (Vol X)
The Reiki Master's Manual (Vol XI)

ADULT COLORING JOURNALS
SERIES-ZEN COLORING:
Quantum Energy and Mindful Living Journal (Vol 1)
Reiki Energy Journal (Vol 2)
Nine Spiritual Gifts Journal (Vol 3)
I Forgive Journal (Vol 4)

SERIES – COLORING PROSPERITY:
Genie-Inspired Mandalas and Wealth Journal (Vol 1)
Entrepreneurial Mindset Reboot (Vol 2)

SERIES – HARMONIC MIND CODE:
Harmonic Mind Code Coloring Journal (Vol 1)

FOR CHILDREN
I am Big Tonight. I Don't Need the Light

Dedicated

to my great, great, great, great… grandaunt, Costanza Farnese

Illegitimate Grace

Costanza Farnese: A Legacy of Power, Resilience, and Love

Born in 1500 to Alessandro Farnese—an ambitious cardinal who would later ascend to the papacy as Pope Paul III—and Silvia Ruffini, a noblewoman of rare beauty and steadfast resolve, Costanza Farnese came into the world at the intersection of privilege and secrecy. As the illegitimate daughter of a cleric navigating the halls of Renaissance power, Costanza's life was shaped by both the opportunities and burdens of her lineage.

Raised in the shadow of the Vatican, Costanza experienced firsthand the opulence and intrigue of Renaissance Rome. Her mother, Silvia, ensured that her education matched her noble bloodline, instilling in her a deep intellect, diplomatic acumen, and an innate sense of propriety. Yet, the whispers of her illegitimacy followed her, casting a shadow over the privileges afforded by her father's recognition.

Alessandro's ambitions propelled the Farnese family to prominence, and Costanza played a pivotal role in securing their legacy. Her marriage to Bosio Sforza, Count of Santa Fiora, united two powerful dynasties, tethering her fate to the rolling hills of Tuscany and the complex feudal politics of central Italy. Together, they forged a partnership that was equal parts love and strategy, raising children who would carry forward their family's influence.

Costanza's life was marked by trials that would have broken lesser spirits. The sudden death of her beloved Bosio left her as the matriarch of the Sforza household, a role she embraced with unwavering determination. Amidst political unrest, personal loss, and the ever-present demands of her family's ambition, Costanza proved herself a formidable leader. She navigated bandit uprisings, contentious alliances, and the weight of her children's futures with grace and fortitude.

Her story unfolds against the backdrop of momentous events: the rise of her father as Pope Paul III, the Counter-Reformation, the turmoil of Renaissance Italy, and the enduring power struggles of the Farnese family. Yet, it is not only a tale of politics and power. Costanza's life is a testament to resilience and sacrifice, a balance of duty and love, and a woman's quiet yet profound strength in shaping her family's legacy.

Costanza Farnese's legacy endures in the annals of history and the hearts of those who remember her. She was a woman who, though born under the veil of illegitimacy, transcended the limitations of her time to leave a mark on her family, her country, and the world.

The threads of our past weave a
tapestry we cannot escape, yet within
its design lies the strength to shape
our own destiny.

Dr. Constance Santego

Fact:

All historical references, events, and societal customs depicted in this novel are inspired by real people, places, and eras, though some have been adapted to fit the narrative and characters. This story was crafted with inspiration to offer you, the reader, a fresh perspective, a new way to understand history, and an opportunity to reflect on the complexities of legacy, identity, and empowerment.

While many locations and all personal characters are fictionalized, the essence of their world remains rooted in the truths of Renaissance Italy.

Prologue

In the gilded halls of Renaissance Rome, shadows and light danced in equal measure, reflecting the splendor and secrets of a city where faith and ambition intertwined. Here, power was both a blessing and a curse, and names carried the weight of empires—or the sting of whispered scandal.

I was born into this world of contradictions. The daughter of a noblewoman whose beauty could command a room and a man sworn to the Church, I came into existence not as a celebration, but as a secret. My father, Alessandro Farnese, was destined for greatness, his ambition carved into every stone of the Farnese name. My mother, Silvia Ruffini, carried her grace like armor, shielding us from the harsh judgment of a society that measured worth by lineage and legitimacy.

Yet, even secrets have power. By the time my father ascended to the papacy as Pope Paul III, I had learned that shadows can hide more than shame—they can protect, empower, and even illuminate. In those shadows, I found my strength.

This is not the story of kings and popes, though their voices echo through its pages. This is the story of a woman born at the edge of power, forced to navigate its tempestuous waters. It is the story of alliances forged and broken, of loyalty tested and courage found.

Most of all, it is the story of a name. A name that carried me into palaces and into battlefields of politics, a name that whispered my worth and defied my existence all at once: Farnese.

Before you judge me, walk with me. Before you condemn the choices of the past, consider the price we paid.

Chapter 1

Rome, 1500

The air in the Ruffini villa was heavy with the scent of burning herbs and desperation. Outside, the city bustled, oblivious to the secret unfolding behind the thick stone walls. Inside, the only sounds were muffled cries and the hurried whispers of midwives moving like ghosts through the dimly lit chamber. A storm brewed on the horizon, its distant thunder rolling like the judgment of heaven itself.

Silvia Ruffini clutched the edge of the bed, her face pale but resolute. She had endured hours of pain in silence, refusing to scream. This birth, though natural, was anything but ordinary. The child she carried was a gift, yes, but also a burden—a fragile link between love and scandal, between power and ruin.

"Push, my lady," the midwife urged, her voice steady despite the tension in the room. Beside her, an older woman, the healer, muttered prayers under her breath, calling upon the Virgin Mary for mercy.

Silvia gritted her teeth and pushed, her mind flickering to thoughts of Alessandro Farnese. He had promised to come before the birth, to be there in the hours when their fates entwined most closely. But he was not here. His world was one of holy walls and whispered corridors, of crimson robes and unspoken oaths. And hers—a villa cloaked in shadows, where love and discretion met in equal measure.

A final push brought a cry—sharp, alive, defiant. The room stilled as the midwife held up the infant, her face a mixture of relief and awe.

"A daughter," she whispered, her voice reverent. "A strong one."

Silvia's arms reached instinctively, trembling as the midwife placed the child in her embrace. The baby's cries quieted as Silvia held her close, her heart swelling with love and trepidation. "Costanza," she murmured, the name a whispered promise. It meant constancy, a steadfastness that Silvia prayed would guide her daughter through the trials that awaited her.

The storm outside drew closer, the sound of rain beginning to patter against the villa's windows. Costanza stirred in her mother's arms, her tiny face scrunching before settling into quiet contentment. Silvia's gaze shifted to the window, where the dark clouds loomed.

Alessandro would come. He always did. And though he would not be here to hold his daughter in these first moments, Silvia knew his promise to protect them all would remain unbroken. The secret passage beneath the Vatican was his lifeline to her, and it would serve them again, as it always had.

The storm outside finally broke, rain pounding against the windows as lightning split the sky. Costanza Farnese's first cries rose above the thunder, a fitting herald for a life destined to challenge the very fabric of her world. Silvia leaned back against the pillows, her arms cradling Costanza. This child, born in the midst of shadows, would have to navigate a world of light and darkness alike. Silvia pressed a kiss to the baby's head, whispering a prayer she had held in her heart for years.

"You are loved, my child. And you will be strong."

Chapter 2

Beneath Rome's grandeur, a labyrinth of secrets wound its way through the earth like veins, pulsing with whispers of power and indiscretion. In one such passage, cloaked in darkness, a man moved swiftly, his crimson robes brushing the damp walls as torchlight flickered over ancient stone. Alessandro Farnese, cardinal of the Holy Church, carried the weight of his dual life in his stride. Above ground, he was a man of God. Below, in the hidden corridors that connected the Vatican to the Ruffini villa, he was simply a man—a father rushing to meet his newborn child.

The air was damp, heavy with the scent of stone and earth, and the faint echo of his footsteps seemed to chase him. The passage, centuries old, had been carved by hands long forgotten, its original purpose lost to time. Now, it served as a lifeline, a hidden artery connecting two worlds that should never have met.

At last, Alessandro reached the concealed entrance. A quick knock in a specific rhythm, and the heavy door creaked open. A trusted servant stood on the other side, bowing his head. "Your Eminence, Lady Ruffini, awaits you."

Alessandro stepped into the villa, brushing droplets of condensation from his robe. "Is the child born?" he asked, his voice sharp with urgency.

The servant nodded. "A daughter, my lord. Both mother and child are well."

Relief flickered across Alessandro's face, softening the lines etched by years of ambition and secrecy. He moved quickly through the villa's quiet corridors, the faint cries of a newborn guiding his steps. At the door to the birthing chamber, he hesitated, placing a hand on the worn wood. Inside, his family awaited him—a reality that both grounded and complicated his life.

He pushed the door open.

Silvia looked up from her place on the bed, her face still pale but illuminated by a quiet strength. Cradled in her arms was the smallest of bundles, a tiny face peeking out from the folds of soft linen.

"It's done," Silvia said softly. "Costanza is here."

Alessandro crossed the room, his footsteps measured, his presence filling the space. He paused beside the bed, looking down at the child who now held a piece of his heart. She was so small, her tiny fist curling instinctively as if ready to grasp the world. A faint smile tugged at his lips.

"She's beautiful," he said, his voice barely above a whisper. He reached out a hand, his fingers brushing the baby's head with a gentleness that seemed at odds with his formidable presence. For a moment, the burdens of his position faded, leaving only the fragile joy of fatherhood.

Silvia studied him carefully. "And what of her future? What of the life she will lead? You know what they will say—about me, about her."

Alessandro's expression darkened, his gaze resting on the tiny bundle in Silvia's arms. His daughter, born into both privilege and shadow, would bear the weight of whispers alone—for now. Her existence, a blessing to him, would be seen by others as a weapon to undermine his standing. She would carry the burden of his choices, but she would also be his legacy.

"She will be protected," he said firmly. "I will ensure it."

Silvia's brow furrowed. "Protection is not enough. She needs more than that. She needs a place in this world, a name that carries weight and shields her from judgment."

Alessandro straightened, the commanding air of a cardinal settling over him. "Her name will be her shield. Costanza Farnese. She will not be hidden. She will not be denied."

The words hung heavy in the air, a promise and a challenge. Costanza stirred slightly in Silvia's arms, her tiny hand curling into a fist as if ready to face the world. Alessandro's gaze softened as he looked at her. "You are my legacy," he said quietly. "One day, you will carry our name into the future. But you must do so wisely, with courage."

Silvia watched him closely, her fingers brushing against Costanza's tiny hand. "And what of the Church? What of those who would see you fall for the life you've chosen?"

Alessandro's jaw tightened, but his resolve remained unshaken. "The world may know of her existence, but it will not know the details of our lives. This passage protects us from prying eyes and keeps what remains sacred within these walls. Discretion is our shield, Silvia. It always has been."

The storm outside reached its peak, rain lashing against the windows as thunder echoed through the villa. Alessandro turned back to his daughter, the weight of his promises settling heavily on his shoulders. Costanza stirred in Silvia's arms, her tiny face scrunching before softening into peace.

"She will be strong," he said, more to himself than anyone else. "Born in shadow, perhaps, but destined for light."

Silvia met his gaze, her own resolve matching his. "Then let her light guide us all."

As the storm began to recede, the Ruffini villa fell into an uneasy stillness. Alessandro stood for a moment longer, his hand resting lightly on Costanza's head. Then, with a final glance at his family, he turned and disappeared into the corridors once more, the secrets of the passage wrapping around him like a cloak.

Above, the city of Rome carried on, unaware of the life born in its shadows—a life that would one day rise to meet its destiny.

Chapter 3

The years passed swiftly within the walls of the Ruffini villa, the rhythm of life dictated by seasons and secrets. Costanza Farnese grew into a curious, determined child, her world shaped by warmth, privilege, and the quiet unease that came with being a daughter of shadow. By the age of ten, she had become acutely aware of the duality of her existence—a cherished child within the villa but a whispered scandal beyond its walls.

It was a crisp autumn morning when Costanza stood in the courtyard, her wooden practice sword clutched tightly in her hand. She faced no opponent, only the air, her movements deliberate and fierce. The olive trees surrounding the courtyard swayed gently in the breeze, their golden leaves catching the sunlight.

"You'll wear yourself out before you learn anything," Silvia called from the doorway, a wry smile softening her features.

Costanza paused mid-strike, lowering the sword. "I need to be strong," she said, turning to face her mother. "Father says it's important."

Silvia approached, her skirts brushing the cobblestones. "Your father says many things, my dear. But strength comes in many forms. It's not just about swords and fighting."

Costanza frowned, her hazel eyes sharp with determination. "But people talk about us. About him. I've heard them."

Silvia's smile faltered. She knelt to meet her daughter's gaze, brushing a stray lock of hair from Costanza's face. "What have you heard?"

"They say we don't belong," Costanza replied, her voice steady despite the hurt behind her words. "They call me a bastard. They say Father has no right to be a cardinal."

Silvia's heart ached at the pain in her daughter's voice. "People will always talk," she said softly. "They will always find reasons to judge. But their words do not define you. What defines you is how you choose to carry yourself."

Costanza tilted her head, searching her mother's face for answers. "But why do they hate us? Why do they judge him?"

Silvia hesitated, weighing her words. "Your father's life is complicated, Costanza. He is a man of great responsibility and ambition, and not everyone understands the choices he's made. But know this—he loves you, more than anything. And his love will always protect you."

Costanza's grip on the sword tightened. "I want to protect him too."

~

That evening, as the sun dipped below the horizon and the villa was bathed in the soft glow of candlelight, Costanza sat by the hearth, her thoughts far from the book in her lap.

"Mother," she said suddenly, breaking the quiet.

Silvia looked up from her embroidery. "Yes, my dear?"

"Why does Father come so rarely?"

Silvia paused, her needle hovering above the fabric. She had prepared for this question, but that didn't make it easier to answer. "Your father is a man of great responsibility, Costanza. His work for the Church requires much of his time."

"But he's also our father," Costanza said, her voice tinged with frustration. "Doesn't that matter?"

Silvia set her embroidery aside and moved to sit beside her daughter. "Of course it matters," she said gently. "Your father loves you. All of you. But his love comes with sacrifices. That is the nature of the life he chose."

Costanza frowned. "I didn't choose this life."

"No," Silvia said softly. "But you have the power to shape it. Remember that."

For a moment, the only sound was the crackle of the fire. Then Costanza leaned into her mother's side, her voice barely above a whisper. "I'll make him proud. I promise."

Silvia wrapped her arms around her daughter, holding her close. "You already do, my love."

~

The years would test that promise, but for now, it was enough. Costanza closed her eyes, letting the warmth of her mother's embrace and the flickering fire carry her into dreams. Outside, the world awaited—a world that would challenge her, define her, and, one day, bow to her.

Chapter 4

Rome, 1511

The early morning light cast a golden hue over the Eternal City, illuminating its contradictions. Crumbling ruins from the age of emperors stood side by side with grand Renaissance palaces and churches, symbols of the city's rebirth. Narrow streets bustled with life as merchants called out to potential customers, their voices mixing with the sound of pilgrims offering prayers, artisans crafting their wares, and the distant toll of church bells. Above it all loomed St. Peter's Basilica, its unfinished dome a reminder of both the Church's grandeur and its ambitions.

From the window of her villa, Costanza Farnese gazed out at the city that seemed both familiar and impossibly vast. To a young girl of eleven, Rome was a mystery—its streets alive with opportunity but shadowed by secrets. She could see the dome of St. Peter's Basilica in the distance, towering over the rooftops like a silent sentinel. Her father was often there, she knew, navigating the intricate web of power and faith that ruled the Catholic world.

A Church Divided

Costanza turned as her mother, Silvia, entered the room, a letter in hand. "From your father," Silvia said, her voice steady but her expression tired. "He writes of the Vatican."

Costanza's curiosity was immediate. "What does he say?"

Silvia sat beside her daughter, smoothing the folds of her gown as she spoke. "The Church is restless," she began. "Your father writes of tensions—within the Vatican, within Rome, within the faith itself."

Costanza furrowed her brow. "How can a church be restless? Isn't it supposed to be... peaceful?"

Silvia smiled faintly. "In theory, yes. But in truth, the Church is made up of men, and men are rarely at peace." She paused, her gaze drifting toward the distant Vatican. "There are those who see corruption in the Church's wealth, in the indulgences sold to fund its projects. There are others who believe it has strayed too far from its purpose. Your father is careful, Costanza. He must be, in such times."

Costanza listened intently, though she didn't fully understand. She only knew that her father was part of something larger than their family—something that seemed both powerful and fragile. "Is it dangerous?" she asked quietly.

Silvia hesitated. "Not yet. But change is coming, my dear. Rome feels it, even if it cannot name it."

The Vatican's Ambition

Later that day, Costanza wandered the villa's gardens, her thoughts filled with the stories her mother had shared. She imagined her father walking the hallowed halls of the Vatican, surrounded by other cardinals in their crimson robes. She had heard of Pope Julius II, the "Warrior Pope," who had waged wars and commissioned artists to leave their mark on Rome. Her father had spoken of Michelangelo, who was painting a ceiling in the Sistine Chapel, and of the grand plans to rebuild St. Peter's Basilica.

The Vatican's ambitions fascinated her. It was a place of art, of faith, of unimaginable power. But it was also a place of conflict. She had overheard whispers among the servants—rumors of intrigue, of rivalries, of schemes played out in the shadows. Costanza wasn't sure what to make of it all. She only knew that the Vatican's walls hid as much as they revealed.

The Streets of Rome

One afternoon, Silvia allowed Costanza to accompany her to the market. The streets were alive with activity—merchants from the East selling spices, Spanish soldiers strolling with a swagger, German artisans demonstrating their skills. Costanza loved the colors and smells, the endless variety of people and goods.

Yet even here, the Church was present. Priests moved among the crowd, offering blessings and collecting alms. Pilgrims knelt in prayer, their faces etched with devotion and exhaustion. And above it all, the Vatican's presence loomed, a reminder of who truly held power in Rome.

"Do you see it, Costanza?" Silvia asked, her tone thoughtful. "The city is a reflection of the Church itself. Beautiful, complex, and divided."

Costanza didn't respond. She was watching a group of children playing near the market's edge. One of them shouted something, and the others laughed, the sound carrying over the clamor of the crowd. She felt a pang of longing—for what, she couldn't quite say. Perhaps for a simpler life, one unbound by the expectations and whispers that followed her family.

A City of Secrets

That evening, as the sun dipped below the horizon, Costanza sat by the fire with her mother. The flickering light cast long shadows on the walls, and the villa seemed suddenly vast and quiet.

"Mother," she said, breaking the silence, "Are there really tunnels under the city? Ones that go to the Vatican?"

Silvia glanced at her daughter, her expression unreadable. "Who told you that?"

"I heard the servants talking," Costanza admitted. "They said Father uses them."

Silvia sighed. "There are passages, yes. They are ancient, built long before us. But what your father uses them for is no concern of yours."

Costanza frowned. "But doesn't it mean he has secrets?"

"Everyone has secrets," Silvia said gently. "Even you, one day."

Costanza looked into the fire, her thoughts racing. Rome was a city of secrets, that much she understood. And her family was no exception. She wondered how many more truths lay hidden beneath the city, beneath her father's careful words and her mother's guarded smile.

As the fire crackled and the night deepened, Costanza felt a growing awareness of the world around her—a world of faith and ambition, of beauty and danger. It was a world she was just beginning to understand, and one she would one day claim as her own.

Chapter 5

The halls of the Vatican shimmered with opulence, their marble floors polished to a gleam that reflected the light of towering candelabras. Even at eleven years old, Costanza Farnese could sense the weight of the history embedded in the walls, the air thick with power and purpose. She moved carefully, her slippers making barely a sound as she followed the familiar corridor that led to her father's private meeting chamber.

Costanza wasn't supposed to be here. She knew that. But curiosity, coupled with a longing to see Cardinal Alessandro Farnese, her father, had gotten the better of her. He had been away from the villa for weeks, his duties in Rome consuming him entirely. When Costanza overheard a servant mention that he would be at the Vatican all afternoon, she had resolved to see him—if only for a moment.

Her small figure slipped unnoticed past the Swiss Guards stationed at the entrance. They were too preoccupied with their rigid postures and ceremonial halberds to notice the determined girl weaving through the shadows. Costanza had visited the Vatican once before, during a grand procession, but the corridors had felt entirely different then—filled with priests, diplomats, and nobles in their finest attire. Now, the silence seemed almost eerie, broken only by the distant murmur of voices.

As she approached her father's chamber, Costanza slowed her pace. The door was ajar, and through the narrow gap, she could see him standing with his back to her, his crimson robes a stark contrast to the gilded walls. Opposite him stood a man she recognized from his portraits: Pope Julius II, his presence as formidable as the rumors suggested.

Their voices, low and serious, carried through the opening.

"The League of Cambrai has fractured," Julius said, his tone edged with frustration. "Venice is no longer our primary concern. The King of France grows bolder with each passing day, and I will not have his ambition threaten the Church."

Costanza furrowed her brow. She knew little about France, other than it was a distant place ruled by a king. But her father's response piqued her interest further.

"Your Holiness," Alessandro said calmly, "The Farnese estates remain loyal, as do many others in Italy. But if France aligns with Milan or the Holy Roman Empire, their combined strength could challenge even Rome. Diplomacy must take precedence before war becomes inevitable."

Julius scoffed, pacing the room with surprising energy for a man of his age. "Diplomacy?" he snapped. "There is no diplomacy with wolves, Farnese. Only strength will deter them. And you—your family's position in Latium is strategic. Do not forget that."

Costanza's heart raced as she listened, her young mind struggling to piece together the weight of their conversation. Wars, alliances, France—these were words she had heard before but never understood fully. Yet the tension in their voices was unmistakable, a palpable force that hung in the room like the heavy scent of incense.

Lost in her thoughts, Costanza barely noticed the approaching footsteps until it was too late. A figure loomed behind her, clearing his throat. Startled, she spun around to see a tall priest staring down at her. His expression caught between surprise and disapproval.

"What are you doing here, child?" he whispered harshly. "This is no place for you."

"I—I'm sorry," Costanza stammered, her cheeks flushing. "I only wanted to see my father."

Before the priest could respond, Alessandro's voice called from inside the chamber. "Who is there?"

The priest stepped through the door, pulling Costanza gently but firmly by the arm. "Cardinal Farnese," he began, "This child—"

"Costanza?" Alessandro's voice, though stern, carried a note of surprise. He turned, his sharp gaze softening slightly as he took in her small, apologetic figure. "What are you doing here?"

She lowered her head, her voice trembling. "I wanted to see you, Father. I didn't mean to interrupt."Pope Julius, who had been silent until now, let out a low chuckle. "Well, Farnese, it seems your ambitions are not the only thing that follows you into the Vatican."Alessandro stepped forward, his expression unreadable. He knelt before Costanza, placing a hand gently on her shoulder. "You should not be here, my child," he said quietly. "This is a place of great responsibility, and the matters discussed here are not for young ears." "I'm sorry," she whispered, her eyes welling with tears. "I just wanted to hear your voice. You've been gone so long."

Her words seemed to pierce through Alessandro's stoic exterior. For a moment, he said nothing, only brushing a strand of hair from her face. Then he straightened, his tone softening. "I will escort her back to the entrance," he said to Julius, who waved a dismissive hand.

"Go, Farnese," Julius said. "We'll continue this later. It seems your daughter has reminded us that even the most ambitious men are still fathers."

The walk through the Vatican corridors was silent at first, Alessandro's robes brushing softly against the marble as Costanza struggled to keep pace. She wanted to speak, to explain herself, but the weight of his presence kept her quiet.

Finally, he stopped near a carved doorway, turning to face her. "Costanza," he said, his voice low but kind. "You are my daughter, and I will always make time for you. But there are things in this world—things I must do—that you cannot yet understand."

She nodded, biting her lip. "I only wanted to see you," she said again, her voice small.

"And you have," he replied, his expression softening. "But you must trust me. There is a time for everything, and your time to understand will come."

He bent down, pressing a kiss to her forehead. "Now, go home with Lorenzo and stay out of trouble. I'll return to the villa soon."

As she was led away by a waiting servant, Costanza glanced back, her young heart heavy with questions. She didn't understand everything she had heard in that chamber, but one thing was clear: her father's world was one of immense power and danger, a world she longed to be part of but couldn't yet grasp. The image of him standing beside Pope Julius II stayed with her, a reminder of the man who was both her father and something far greater.

Chapter 6

Rome 1513

The Palazzo della Cancelleria, a magnificent Renaissance palace near the Vatican, was abuzz with anticipation. Lanterns lined its marble staircases, their golden glow reflecting on the polished walls. Inside, the grand ballroom had been transformed into a spectacle of elegance. Rich tapestries depicting scenes from Roman history adorned the walls, and intricate chandeliers sparkled above, casting a warm glow over the gathered nobility.

Tonight's event was hosted by the Orsini family, one of Rome's most influential noble houses, and served as both a political gathering and a celebration of the season's new debuts. Among the glittering crowd of dignitaries, merchants, and diplomats, Costanza Farnese stood on the precipice of her own introduction to noble society.

~

Earlier at the Ruffini villa, Silvia oversaw every detail of her daughter's appearance. Costanza stood before a tall mirror in her chambers, her reflection framed by soft candlelight. Her gown, a masterpiece of emerald silk, shimmered with gold embroidery at the hem and sleeves. A delicate necklace of pearls rested at her collarbone, accentuating her refined features.

"You look beautiful, my dear," Silvia said, adjusting the ribbon tied around Costanza's waist. "Tonight is an important night—not just for you, but for all of us."

Costanza tried to steady her breathing, her nerves building as the moment drew closer. "What if I say the wrong thing? Or forget my curtsy?"

"You won't," Silvia assured her. "You've been preparing for this. Remember to listen carefully, speak graciously, and smile when it matters. You are a Farnese."

The mention of her father's name made Costanza's stomach tighten. Though Alessandro Farnese had returned to Rome in recent weeks, she saw him only briefly, his time consumed by meetings and audiences. Tonight, however, he would be present—watching, judging, and no doubt already considering the alliances this night might secure.

The Farnese family arrived at the palazzo in a gleaming carriage drawn by four white horses. Costanza sat beside her mother while Pier Luigi, now a confident ten-year-old, watched the bustling streets of Rome through the window. Their father had traveled ahead, no doubt, to confer with other cardinals and dignitaries.

As they stepped into the entrance hall, Costanza was struck by the sheer scale of the gathering. Laughter and music floated through the air, mingling with the hum of conversation. Women in gowns of rich brocade and men in velvet doublets adorned with gold and jewels filled the space, their presence a testament to Rome's wealth and power.

At the head of the room stood Cardinal Alessandro Farnese, his crimson robes lending him an aura of authority. He caught Costanza's eye and gave her a brief nod—approval or perhaps expectation. She wasn't sure which.

Costanza's heart raced as she approached the main hall, her hand resting lightly on Pier Luigi's arm. The master of ceremonies, a man with a booming voice and an impressive mustache, announced her arrival to the gathered guests.

"Lady Costanza Farnese, daughter of Cardinal Alessandro Farnese," he proclaimed.

All eyes turned toward her, their gazes a mix of curiosity and admiration. Costanza forced herself to breathe, to remember the countless lessons in decorum and poise. She dipped into a graceful curtsy, her skirts fanning out around her, and offered a polite smile as she rose.

A ripple of approval moved through the crowd. She had done it. The first step was over.

The evening passed in a flurry of introductions and conversations. Costanza met ambassadors from Spain and France, Roman senators, and Venetian merchants, each one assessing her with subtle glances and veiled questions. She responded with the careful elegance her mother had taught her, though she couldn't help but feel the weight of every word.

At one point, she found herself standing beside her father. Alessandro introduced her to Count Giovanni della Rovere, an older man with sharp eyes and a calculating smile.

"Lady Costanza," the count said, his tone formal but curious. "It is a pleasure to meet the daughter of such a distinguished man. Tell me, do you enjoy life in Rome?"

Costanza hesitated, aware of the expectations behind the question. "Rome is a city of great beauty and history, my lord," she said carefully. "It is both inspiring and humbling."

The count nodded, seemingly satisfied with her answer. "Wise words for one so young. You will do well, I think."

Her father gave her a faint smile—a rare expression of approval. Costanza allowed herself a moment of relief before being swept away into another conversation.

Later in the evening, the string ensemble struck up a lively tune, and the floor cleared for dancing. Costanza hesitated at the edge of the crowd, unsure whether she should join. Before she could decide, a young man with dark curls and a confident smile approached.

"May I have the honor of this dance, Lady Costanza?" he asked, bowing low.

She glanced toward her mother, who gave a subtle nod. Taking the young man's offered hand, she allowed herself to be led onto the floor. The dance was a stately pavane, with slow, deliberate movements that gave her time to observe her partner.

"You are handling tonight well," he said, his voice low enough that only she could hear. "Many would find this overwhelming."

"It is overwhelming," Costanza admitted, her tone light. "But I'm glad to have survived so far."

The young man chuckled. "Surviving is the first step. Thriving comes next."

As the evening wore on, Costanza found herself near a group of older noblewomen. Their conversation carried on hushed but animated tones. She pretended to admire a nearby tapestry as she listened.

"Her father is already negotiating," one woman said. "The Sforza family would be a strong match."

"But she's so young," another whispered. "Barely thirteen."

"Young enough to mold, old enough to marry," came the reply.

Costanza's stomach turned. They were talking about her future and her marriage as though she were a commodity to be traded. She stepped away quickly, the words buzzing in her ears.

By the time the evening ended, Costanza felt both exhausted and exhilarated. She had made her debut, navigated the stares and questions, and even earned a nod of approval from her father. But the whispers of negotiation lingered, a reminder of the weight she carried as a Farnese.

As the family returned to their carriage, Alessandro placed a hand on her shoulder. "You did well tonight," he said simply.

"Thank you, Father," she replied, though her thoughts were far from settled. The glittering world of Rome had revealed itself to her that night, full of beauty and intrigue. But it was also a world of expectations, where every smile, every word, carried the weight of ambition.

And for Costanza, the journey had only just begun.

Chapter 7

Costanza sat by the open window of the villa's library, the warm summer breeze rustling the parchment of an unfinished letter on the desk before her. From below, the faint sound of her brothers sparring in the courtyard floated upward, their laughter punctuated by the clatter of wooden swords. Yet her attention was drawn to the voices carrying through the stone walls from her father's study.

She recognized the low, deliberate tones of Cardinal Alessandro Farnese, though the voice of her mother, Silvia Ruffini, was softer, more cautious. Costanza leaned closer to the window, straining to make out their words.

Inside the study, Alessandro paced back and forth, his crimson robes brushing the marble floor. Silvia sat at the edge of a chaise, her hands folded neatly in her lap, her eyes tracking her companion with concern.

"This is no ordinary transition," Alessandro said, his voice tight with frustration. "The death of Pope Julius II has thrown everything into uncertainty."

"And Pope Leo?" Silvia asked gently. "Does he not bring stability?"

Alessandro paused, his gaze sharp. "Stability, yes, but at what cost? Leo is a Medici, through and through. His priorities are his family's power, not the Church's sanctity. Already, the coffers are being drained for his indulgences and those infernal festivals. Rome is at risk of losing respect, Silvia, and I cannot afford to be associated with a Papacy seen as decadent and weak."

Silvia tilted her head slightly, her voice measured. "You speak as though you disagree with his methods. Yet, isn't that how power is wielded here? Through influence, wealth, and alliances?"

Alessandro sighed, stopping at the window to gaze out over the courtyard. "It is how power is taken. But it must also be maintained. Leo gambles with the Church's credibility. If he is not careful, it will fracture further. The discontent with indulgences grows louder every day, from Germany to England."

"Martin Luther," Silvia said quietly.

"Yes, Luther," Alessandro said, his voice laced with disdain. "An Augustinian monk stirring trouble in Wittenberg, questioning the very foundation of our faith. His words are dangerous, Silvia. He is no mere reformer—he is a firebrand. And if Leo does not act decisively, that fire will spread."

At the mention of Martin Luther, Costanza's ears perked up. She had heard whispers of the monk's name before, though she knew little of his actions. Something about indulgences and sermons, spoken in hushed tones by the villa's servants. Now, hearing her father's urgency, she realized this man was more than a distant figure—he was a threat to the world her father inhabited.

Her mother's voice broke through her thoughts. "And where do you stand, Alessandro? You have always balanced ambition with loyalty. How will you navigate this?"

"I will stand where I must to protect our family and the Farnese name," Alessandro replied firmly. "Leo is my ally for now, but alliances shift as the tides do. Julius understood the art of diplomacy through strength; Leo is blinded by his own brilliance."

"And the Farnese?" Silvia asked, her voice soft but pointed. "What of Costanza? Pier Luigi? Are they not part of this strategy?"

Alessandro turned sharply, his eyes narrowing. "They are the strategy, Silvia. Costanza's marriage must solidify our standing. Pier Luigi's training will prepare him for leadership, for land, and for war if necessary. I will not allow our family to be a pawn in the games of others. If anything, we will control the board."

Costanza felt a chill run down her spine. Her father's words were clear, even to her young ears: they were all part of his larger plan. She wasn't just his daughter—she was a piece in a vast game of power and survival. Yet her curiosity about this "game" only deepened. What was happening within the Church that caused her father such concern? Who was Martin Luther, and why did he matter so much to Rome?

Her thoughts were interrupted by the sound of footsteps. Costanza quickly moved from the window and feigned interest in the letter on the desk. Moments later, her father entered the library, his expression softened but weary.

"Costanza," he said, his tone neutral. "Have you finished your studies for the day?"

"Yes, Father," she replied quickly, though her heart still raced.

Alessandro stepped closer, placing a hand on her shoulder. "You'll attend an event soon, one of importance. Many people will look to you as a representation of this family. You must be ready."

"I will," Costanza promised, though the weight of his words pressed heavily on her. "Father?"

"Yes?"

"Who is Martin Luther?" she asked, her voice steady but curious.

Alessandro's eyes narrowed slightly, studying her. "A man whose actions you need not concern yourself with. Focus on what is within your control, Costanza. The world will always have men like him, questioning and challenging. It is not for us to indulge their provocations."

He straightened, his commanding presence returning. "Remember: strength and composure. Those are the virtues of a Farnese."

As Alessandro exited, Costanza sat in silence, her mind swirling with questions. She was no stranger to the complexities of her father's world, but tonight, she had glimpsed its deeper shadows. The Church, the Papacy, the politics of power—all of it was larger than she could fully comprehend. Yet, for the first time, she felt the stirrings of a desire to understand.

That evening, as Costanza lay in bed, the words she had overheard replayed in her mind. The Church her father served was not the serene and holy institution she had imagined as a child. It was a battleground, a place where faith and ambition collided. And her family, her name, was deeply entwined in it all.

She stared at the ceiling, the faint glow of moonlight filtering through the curtains. For better or worse, she realized, the Farnese were part of this grand and dangerous game. And so was she.

Chapter 8

Rome, 1515

In the grand halls of the Sforza villa in Rome, Bosio II Sforza moved through the crowd of diplomats, merchants, and nobles with quiet precision. The gathering was one of many his family hosted—a carefully orchestrated display of wealth, influence, and loyalty to the Papal States. Bosio, at 39 years old, carried the weight of the Sforza name on his shoulders, a name intertwined with the shifting power structures of Italy.

The Sforza family, originating from Milan, was no stranger to political intrigue. Though Bosio's branch of the family was not the ruling line of the Duchy of Milan, their influence in Rome was undeniable. They held estates in

Santa Fiora, a region strategically located in Tuscany, and their allegiance to the Church had secured them a foothold in papal politics.

The year 1515 was a time of transition and uncertainty in Rome. Pope Leo X, a Medici, had begun his ambitious projects, draining the Church's treasury to fund extravagant festivals and artistic commissions. Meanwhile, tensions with France and the rumblings of discontent within the Church were shaping the landscape.

For Bosio, Rome was not just a city—it was a battlefield of alliances. The Sforza family's connection to the Papacy was both a blessing and a burden. As a prominent nobleman, Bosio was expected to navigate the complex web of loyalties that bound Rome's elite together, ensuring his family's survival and prosperity in the face of political change.

The Sforzas had risen to prominence during the Renaissance as rulers of Milan, known for their patronage of the arts and their military prowess. Although Bosio's lineage was not directly tied to the ruling seat of Milan, his branch of the family maintained strong connections and influence within the Sforza legacy. This connection made Bosio a valuable ally for the Papal States, which sought to maintain stability in the Italian peninsula amidst growing French aggression.

Bosio himself was a man of pragmatism and diplomacy. While his cousins in Milan were often embroiled in military conflicts, Bosio focused on strengthening his family's position through careful negotiation. His estates in Santa Fiora were a key asset, supplying resources to the Church and serving as a buffer between Rome and the northern territories.

Bosio's relationship with the Papacy deepened in 1515 as Pope Leo X began solidifying his alliances. The Medici pope saw the Sforza family as a crucial partner in balancing the influence of France and the Holy Roman Empire in Italy. Bosio, with his reputation for discretion and loyalty, became a trusted intermediary in negotiations.

For Bosio, this role brought him closer to Cardinal Alessandro Farnese, one of the Church's most ambitious figures. Alessandro, always looking for advantageous alliances, saw potential in linking the Farnese and Sforza families. Though the idea of a marriage to Alessandro's daughter, Costanza, was not yet formalized, discussions about potential unions between noble houses were common in their circles.

On this particular evening, Bosio stood near the edge of the grand hall, his dark eyes scanning the room. The hum of conversation surrounded him—talk of French ambitions, papal decrees, and trade agreements. But his thoughts lingered on his family's future.

He knew what was expected of him. As the head of his branch of the Sforza family, his duty was to ensure its survival and prosperity. Marriage, alliances, and land—these were the tools of power. Yet, he had always approached these responsibilities with caution. Too many of his peers had been consumed by the very ambitions they sought to fulfill.

His thoughts were interrupted by the arrival of a messenger bearing a letter marked with the Farnese seal. Bosio took the parchment, his expression unreadable as he broke the wax seal and scanned the contents.

"Cardinal Farnese," he murmured to himself. The letter spoke of an invitation—a formal meeting to discuss matters of mutual benefit. Though the details were vague, Bosio could read between the lines. Alessandro Farnese, ever the strategist, was laying the groundwork for something significant.

Bosio folded the letter carefully, slipping it into the pocket of his doublet. The Farnese family was ambitious, and their influence grew steadily. Aligning with them could strengthen the Sforzas' position in Rome, but it would also draw him deeper into the labyrinth of papal politics.

As the evening wore on, Bosio found himself standing alone on the villa's terrace, gazing out over the city. The lights of Rome shimmered like stars, a reflection of the city's allure and danger. His mind wandered to the Farnese daughter he had heard of in passing— Costanza, a young woman of fifteen, already navigating the delicate balance between noble expectations and her own burgeoning sense of identity.

He wondered what she was like. Was she as poised and intelligent as her father claimed? Or was she simply another pawn in Alessandro's intricate game? Either way, Bosio knew that his decisions in the coming months would shape the future of both their families.

With a sigh, he straightened his shoulders and returned to the hall. The path ahead was uncertain, but Bosio had spent his life navigating the complexities of power. He would do what was necessary—not just for himself, but for the legacy of the Sforza name.

Chapter 9

The light of early morning spilled through the tall windows of the Ruffini villa, casting golden patterns on the marble floors. Costanza Farnese sat upright at her writing desk, the faint rustle of quills and paper filling the air as her tutor paced behind her. At fifteen, she was no longer a child, and the expectations placed upon her had grown with each passing year.

Her mornings were spent in rigorous study. Under her tutor's watchful eye, she practiced her Latin, copied passages from Cicero, and read aloud from the works of Dante. Education for a young woman of her standing was meant to cultivate grace and intellect, though not to challenge the men who ruled society. Still, Costanza often pressed her tutor with questions.

"Why did Virgil guide Dante through the underworld?" she asked, pausing in her recitation.

Her tutor, a gray-haired man with a stern expression, hesitated. "He was a symbol of reason and wisdom, my lady," he replied. "A guide through chaos."

"But Dante left Virgil behind when he reached paradise," Costanza countered. "Does that mean reason is not enough?"

The tutor raised an eyebrow, clearly unsure how to respond. "It is not your place to question such matters, my lady. Continue."

Costanza bit back a smile, her mind racing with thoughts she dared not speak aloud.

By midmorning, the lessons shifted. Costanza moved to the salon, where a governess awaited her with a new challenge: the art of courtly grace. In Renaissance Rome, a noblewoman's poise and presentation were as crucial as her education. She was taught to walk with her chin high, her back straight, and her hands folded just so. Every movement was deliberate, every gesture a reflection of her status.

"Do not slouch, Costanza," her governess chided as she practiced walking with a book balanced on her head. "You carry the Farnese name. Let the world see your dignity before they hear your words."

Costanza sighed but obeyed. Her mother often reminded her that appearances were everything, especially in a city where whispers carried farther than shouts.

After a light meal, the afternoons were hers—at least in part. On certain days, she accompanied her mother to visit other noblewomen. These gatherings were a careful dance of alliances, gossip, and subtle power plays. Costanza learned early to listen more than she spoke, absorbing the unspoken rules of the social hierarchy.

On quieter days, she wandered the villa gardens or worked on her embroidery, her mind drifting to the stories she read in the mornings. She wondered what it would be like to step beyond the confines of her family's estate, to walk the streets of Rome without the weight of her name.

Her favorite afternoons were those spent with her mother, Silvia, in the villa's library. Silvia often read aloud from the Psalms or told stories of her own childhood. It was during these moments that Costanza felt most at ease, her questions about the world briefly set aside.

As the sun dipped low, her father's shadow loomed larger. Alessandro Farnese, now more entrenched in the Vatican's inner workings, visited the villa less frequently, but his influence was ever-present. On the evenings when he did return, Costanza was expected to sit quietly as he discussed politics and Church matters with her mother.

This evening, she gathered the courage to ask a question.

"Father," she began hesitantly, "Why does the Church concern itself so much with earthly power? Isn't it supposed to guide souls to heaven?"

Alessandro looked at her, his expression unreadable. For a moment, silence hung in the room.

"Because, Costanza," he said finally, setting his goblet of wine on the table, "To guide souls, the Church must first have the power to reach them. The world is not as simple as the stories you read."

Costanza's brow furrowed as she leaned forward, her hands folded neatly in her lap, a habit instilled by her governess. "But why does that power come from gold and armies? Wouldn't faith alone be enough if the Church's purpose is divine?"

Alessandro studied his daughter, his expression unreadable. It was rare for him to have these moments with her, and rarer still for her to challenge him so directly. He glanced at Silvia, seated quietly beside them, her embroidery forgotten in her lap. She gave him a faint, almost imperceptible nod, as if encouraging him to answer.

"Faith," Alessandro began, his tone measured, "Is the foundation of the Church, yes. But faith alone does not build cathedrals. It does not send missionaries to distant lands. It does not defend against those who would see the Church fall."

Costanza tilted her head, her hazel eyes sharp with curiosity. "But does that mean the Church is no different from a kingdom, then? Fighting for land and power?"

Her father's lips pressed into a thin line. "The Church is not a kingdom," he said firmly. "It is a shepherd guiding its flock. But even a shepherd needs a staff to ward off wolves."

"Wolves," Costanza repeated, her voice soft but thoughtful. "Like those who call us names in the markets? Who says the Church is corrupt?"

Alessandro's jaw tightened, but his gaze softened as he looked at her. "Yes," he admitted. "There are wolves among the faithful, and there are wolves outside the Church's gates. Some seek to tear it down because they do not understand it. Others see its flaws and magnify them for their own gain. Power is necessary to protect what is sacred."

Costanza leaned back, her hands loosening in her lap. "But isn't power dangerous too? It can change people. Corrupt them."

Alessandro's eyes narrowed slightly, a flicker of pride mixed with caution crossing his face. "You are wise beyond your years, Costanza. Yes, power is dangerous. That is why it must be wielded carefully, by those who understand its weight."

"And you understand it, Father?" she asked, her voice steady but her gaze questioning.

A faint smile touched his lips, though it did not reach his eyes. "I do what must be done. For the Church. For our family. One day, you will understand that sometimes, doing what is right does not mean doing what is easy."

Silence settled over the room. Costanza's mind raced, her thoughts a tangle of admiration, frustration, and a burgeoning understanding of the world her father navigated. Alessandro picked up his goblet again, taking a measured sip before speaking.

"Tell me," he said, breaking the silence, "What would you do, Costanza? If you were in my place?"

The question caught her off guard. She hesitated, her fingers brushing the edge of her gown as she searched for an answer. "I don't know," she admitted at last. "But I think I would try to be honest."

Alessandro chuckled, a low, weary sound. "Honesty is a luxury few in my position can afford. It is a noble idea, but the truth can be as dangerous as a lie when wielded carelessly."

"Then how do you know what's right?" she asked, her voice tinged with frustration. "If you can't tell the truth, how do you guide anyone?"

He leaned forward, his gaze intent. "You must find the balance, Costanza. You speak the truth when it will build. You withhold it when it will destroy. The Church is both human and divine. It is not perfect, but it is necessary. And so, we must do what is necessary to preserve it."

Costanza met his gaze, her young mind grappling with the weight of his words. For the first time, she saw the man behind the cardinal's robes—not just a father, but a figure navigating a labyrinth of faith and power, sacrifice and ambition.

"I still don't think it's fair," she said quietly.

"Neither do I," he replied, surprising her with his honesty. "But fairness is a luxury, like honesty. And those who seek to shape the world rarely have the privilege of either."

Silvia, who had been listening silently, reached out and placed a hand on Costanza's arm. "Your father's path is not an easy one," she said softly. "But his choices have always been made with us in mind. Remember that."

Costanza nodded slowly, though her questions lingered. As Alessandro stood and bid them goodnight, she watched him go, her heart heavy with newfound understanding. The world was not as simple as she had once believed, and her father was not merely a man of God. He was a man of the world, walking a line between salvation and survival.

As the door closed behind him, Costanza turned back to her mother. "Do you think he's happy?" she asked.

Silvia smiled faintly, sadness flickering in her eyes. "Happiness is not what drives your father," she said. "He is driven by purpose. And for men like him, that is enough."

Costanza stared into the fire, her thoughts swirling. Purpose. Power. Truth. She didn't yet understand how they fit together, but she vowed to learn. One day, she would walk the same line her father did. And when that day came, she would be ready.

His words stayed with her, a reminder of the complex world she would one day navigate.

As the villa settled into quiet, Costanza sat by her window, staring out at the lights of Rome. She thought about her place in the world—the expectations, the rules, and the whispers that seemed to follow her family wherever they went. She knew her life was one of privilege, but it was also one of limitations.

Her mind wandered beyond the marble halls of her home, beyond the walls of the Vatican, to a future she could barely imagine. Costanza Farnese was a young lady now, but in her heart, she was something more—a dreamer, a thinker, and, perhaps, something the world was not yet ready for.

Chapter 10

The villa's garden was a sanctuary, a place where Costanza Farnese could escape the weight of expectations that seemed to grow heavier with each passing year. The faint scent of jasmine and lavender mingled with the crisp autumn air as she stood by the marble fountain at the center of the courtyard. The sun cast long, golden shadows across the cobblestones, illuminating the edges of her gown and her neatly braided hair. At fifteen, she had grown into a young woman of grace and intelligence, her sharp mind both an asset and a source of frustration in a world that expected her to remain silent.

"Costanza!" her mother's voice broke through her thoughts, firm yet unhurried. Silvia Ruffini stood in the doorway, her commanding presence framed by the afternoon light. "Your lessons are waiting."

With a sigh, Costanza smoothed her skirts and turned toward the villa. Lessons filled her mornings and afternoons: Latin recitations, embroidery that tested her patience, and endless lectures on decorum and propriety. She was taught to sit upright, to speak only when spoken to, and to navigate the unspoken rules of noble society with precision.

But lately, there had been something else—a tension in the household that whispered of change. In the quiet moments between lessons, Costanza had overheard servants murmuring about alliances and marriage. Though no one had spoken to her directly, she could feel the invisible strings of her future being pulled, tightening with each passing day.

That evening, the dining hall was lit with the warm glow of candles, their flickering light reflecting off the polished silverware and the deep crimson of her father's robes. Alessandro Farnese had returned to the villa after months of absence, his presence filling the room like a gust of wind. He sat at the head of the table, his hands resting on the armrests of his chair as he surveyed his family.

"Costanza," he said, his voice low but resonant, drawing her attention immediately.

"Yes, Father?" she replied, setting down her fork with practiced poise.

"You are nearly of age," Alessandro began, his gaze steady. "It is time we spoke of your future."

Her pulse quickened, though she kept her expression calm. "My future?" she echoed, her voice betraying only the faintest note of apprehension.

Alessandro leaned back slightly, his posture relaxed yet deliberate. "I have been negotiating with the Sforza family," he said. "Bosio II Sforza is an honorable man. A union with their house would strengthen our position."

Costanza's stomach tightened. She had expected this moment, but the reality of it pressed against her like the weight of the marble walls that surrounded them. "I see," she said carefully, choosing her words as she had been taught. "And what is my role in this union?"

"To ensure its success," Alessandro replied, his tone matter-of-fact. "You will bring dignity and grace to their family, as you have brought to ours. Your duty, Costanza, is to secure the legacy of the Farnese."

The room seemed to grow quieter, the soft clinking of silverware fading into the background. Costanza glanced at her mother, searching for reassurance. Silvia reached out, placing a gentle hand on her daughter's arm.

"It is a good match," Silvia said softly. "You will have a place of respect, a family of your own."

Costanza nodded slowly, though the words sat uneasily in her chest. Respect. Family. These were the promises. But what of choice? What of love? She had read stories of noblewomen bound by duty, their lives dictated by alliances, and the ambitions of men. She had always wondered if she would feel the same resentment they must have felt. Now she knew.

She said nothing more that evening. As the servants cleared the table, she caught her father watching her, his expression unreadable. Was it pride she saw in his eyes? Or perhaps a flicker of regret?

Chapter 11

Costanza leaned against the balcony railing, the crisp autumn breeze brushing her cheeks as she watched her younger brother, Pier Luigi, sparring in the courtyard below. At twelve, he was already growing into the role their father had envisioned for him. His strikes with the practice sword were sharp, his movements precise, but there was a tension in his shoulders—a sign of impatience that his tutor scolded often.

"Pier Luigi, control your stance!" the tutor barked. "A soldier's strength lies not in haste but in discipline."

Pier Luigi gritted his teeth, adjusting his posture before lunging forward with renewed focus. Costanza couldn't help but smile faintly at his determination.

Behind her, their mother's voice interrupted her thoughts. "He's improving."

Costanza turned to find Silvia standing beside her, her hands folded neatly in front of her. She followed her daughter's gaze to the courtyard below. "Your father believes he will be ready to join the military soon."

"Is that what he wants?" Costanza asked softly, her eyes still on her brother.

Silvia tilted her head slightly, her expression thoughtful. "It is what is expected," she said. "Just as your path is set, so is his."

Costanza frowned but said nothing. She admired Pier Luigi's resolve but wondered if he, too, felt the weight of the Farnese name pressing down on him.

Later that evening, Costanza found Pier Luigi in the sitting room, sprawled across a cushioned chair with his practice sword resting on the floor beside him. His hair was damp with sweat, and a faint bruise darkened his forearm—a souvenir from his earlier training.

"Do you ever stop?" she teased, sinking into a chair across from him.

Pier Luigi looked up, a smirk playing on his lips. "Not if I want to be the best."

"Father would approve," Costanza said, though her tone carried a note of skepticism.

Pier Luigi sat up, leaning forward with his elbows on his knees. "It's not about what Father wants," he said. "It's about what needs to be done. Someone has to secure our family's name."

"And that someone has to be you?" Costanza asked.

Pier Luigi shrugged, his expression serious now. "Why not me? I'm the eldest son. It's my duty."

Costanza studied him, her brow furrowing slightly. "But is it what you want?"

He hesitated, his fingers tracing the edge of the sword at his feet. "Does it matter?" he asked finally. "What I want doesn't change what's expected of me. Besides, it's not so bad. I'll make Father proud."

Costanza smiled faintly, though her heart ached for him. "You already do," she said softly as she got up and left the room.

In the quiet of the villa's library, Costanza found her youngest brother, Ranuccio, seated cross-legged on the floor with a thick tome spread open before him. The soft glow of a nearby lantern illuminated his face, his dark eyes fixed intently on the page. At eight, he was far quieter than his older siblings, his world shaped by the books and ideas that surrounded him.

"Do you even stop for dinner?" Costanza asked, leaning against the doorway.

Ranuccio looked up, a small smile tugging at his lips. "It's not that late," he said, though the half-eaten plate of fruit beside him suggested otherwise.

Costanza crossed the room and lowered herself onto the floor beside him. "What are you reading?" she asked, peering over his shoulder.

"Augustine," he replied. "Father says I need to understand theology if I'm to serve the Church."

Costanza tilted her head, studying her brother's earnest expression. "Do you like it?" she asked.

Ranuccio hesitated, his fingers brushing the edge of the page. "I think so," he said finally. "It's peaceful here."

Costanza smiled faintly, brushing a hand over his hair. "Peace is rare in this family," she said. "Enjoy it while you can."

Ranuccio looked at her, his gaze curious. "Do you think I'll be good at it?" he asked. "At being in the Church?"

"You're thoughtful and kind," Costanza said. "If anyone can bring something good to the Church, it's you."

Ranuccio's smile widened slightly, and he returned his focus to the book. Costanza watched him for a moment longer, her heart swelling with both pride and worry. Her brothers were so different, their paths laid out before them with a certainty she envied. Yet she wondered if they, too, felt the silent pull of their family's expectations, the weight of a legacy they hadn't chosen.

As the villa settled into the stillness of night, Costanza found herself staring out of her window, the distant lights of Rome twinkling against the dark horizon. Pier Luigi's determination, Ranuccio's quiet resolve, her own unspoken questions—all swirled in her mind, a reminder of the delicate balance their family walked.

They were Farnese. That name meant power, responsibility, and sacrifice. Each of them carried it in their own way, their lives woven together by duty and ambition. Yet in the quiet moments, Costanza wondered if there was still space for them to dream beyond the shadows of their legacy.

For now, she held on to the bond she shared with her brothers, knowing that in a world as unpredictable as theirs, family was the one certainty she could cling to.

Chapter 12

The air in Rome was thick with anticipation in 1516. The political chessboard of Italy was shifting once more, as alliances were forged and broken with alarming speed. For the Farnese family, this was a year of careful maneuvering, where every action carried the weight of potential opportunity—or ruin.

At the Ruffini villa, Cardinal Alessandro Farnese sat in his study, surrounded by maps and correspondence. Letters from Venice, Florence, and the Papal States littered the desk, alongside diplomatic missives from France and Spain. Alessandro's rise within the Church continued, but the landscape of Europe demanded vigilance.

"The Concordat of Bologna is a turning point," Alessandro muttered to himself, referencing the recent agreement between Pope Leo X and King Francis I of France. The signing of the concordat gave the French king significant influence over the appointment of bishops and abbots within his kingdom—a blow to papal authority, but one Alessandro believed could be turned to Rome's advantage if handled correctly.

Silvia Ruffini entered the room quietly, her presence as steadying as ever. "You've been here since dawn," she said, placing a cup of wine at his elbow. "The children are asking when you'll join them."

"When the affairs of Europe cease their chaos," Alessandro replied with a faint smile. He gestured to the map. "Francis pushes north. Charles of Spain readies himself for the crown of the Holy Roman Empire. And here we sit, caught in the middle of their ambitions."

Silvia leaned over the desk, her gaze sharp. "And what of our ambitions? Costanza is nearly of age. The Sforza alliance—will it happen?"

"It must," Alessandro said, his tone firm. "Bosio Sforza has proven himself a capable ally, and his family's holdings in Santa Fiora are strategically invaluable. Their influence in Tuscany could strengthen our position against any threats from Florence or Milan. Costanza's marriage will solidify that bond."

~

In another part of the villa, Costanza walked through the garden with her younger brother, Ranuccio, now seven and engrossed in his theological studies. The spring blooms surrounded them, but Costanza's thoughts were far from the beauty of the day.

"Father grows more restless," she said, breaking the silence. "Every time I see him, he's buried in letters or maps."

Ranuccio glanced up from the small prayer book he carried. "He carries the weight of the Church and our family. That's not a small thing."

"And what of us?" Costanza asked. "We're part of this weight too. You're being groomed for the Church, Pier Luigi for the military, and me… to be married."

Ranuccio studied her carefully. "Is it Bosio Sforza that troubles you?"

Costanza paused, her hand brushing the petals of a nearby rose. She had met Sforza only once, during a formal reception the year before. He had been polite, reserved, and entirely unreadable. "I hardly know him," she admitted. "Yet my future is tied to his. How am I supposed to feel about that?"

Ranuccio gave a shy smile. "Maybe one day you'll see why he does what he does. And maybe… maybe Father's plans will be good for you too."

Inside the villa's courtyard, Pier Luigi Farnese practiced swordplay with a tutor. His strikes were strong, his movements precise, but there was a fire in his eyes that spoke of his impatience with lessons.

"You're overreaching," the tutor said, stepping back to correct his form. "Strength alone will not win battles. Strategy wins wars."

Pier Luigi frowned but obeyed, adjusting his stance. "Strength still matters," he muttered under his breath.

Alessandro appeared in the archway, watching his son with a critical eye. "Your tutor is right," he said, stepping forward. "But strength and strategy together make a leader."

Pier Luigi straightened, his expression a mix of pride and defiance. "Will I lead, Father? Or will I merely serve as a pawn?"

Alessandro's gaze softened slightly. "You will lead, Pier Luigi. But leadership requires patience. Your time will come."

By the summer of 1516, the negotiations with the Sforza family were nearly finalized. Letters passed between Alessandro and Bosio Sforza, each missive carefully worded to ensure mutual respect and understanding. Though Costanza was aware of the discussions, the details remained distant to her—a shadow on the edges of her life.

One evening, as the family dined together in the villa's grand hall, Alessandro broke the silence. "We will host the Sforzas soon, when the new palace is complete," he announced, his tone leaving no room for argument. "It is time for them to see the strength of the Farnese family firsthand."

Silvia nodded, her gaze flicking briefly to Costanza. "And Costanza?" she asked.

"She will meet Bosio again," Alessandro said, his eyes fixed on his daughter. "This time, not as a child, but as the woman she is becoming."

Costanza set her fork down, her appetite fading. "And what am I to say to him?"

"Say nothing you do not mean," Alessandro replied. "But show him the grace and intelligence of a Farnese. That will be enough."

As 1516 drew to a close, the Farnese family stood on the precipice of change. Alessandro's ambitions within the Church grew ever larger, with whispers of his name being considered for higher offices. Silvia's steady guidance ensured the household remained strong, even as their children moved closer to the roles set before them.

For Costanza, the coming months would bring new challenges and opportunities. She was no longer the curious girl sneaking through Vatican corridors; she was a young woman on the cusp of a future that both excited and terrified her.

In the distance, the bells of St. Peter's Basilica tolled, a reminder of the world beyond the villa—a world of power, faith, and unrelenting ambition.

Chapter 13

Rome, 1517

The air was thick with the sound of progress: the rhythmic clinking of chisels against stone, the low rumble of carts laden with marble, and the barked commands of foremen overseeing the dozens of laborers who toiled under the midday sun. At the heart of the chaos stood Alessandro Farnese, his crimson robes a stark contrast to the dust-covered workers around him. With his arms crossed and his gaze fixed on the partially constructed walls, he looked every bit the man determined to leave a lasting mark on the city.

Nearby, Costanza watched from beneath the shade of a silk parasol, the heat pressing heavily against her skin despite the light breeze. At seventeen, she was no stranger to her father's grand ambitions, but seeing the palace rise from the earth was something else entirely. It was as if the Farnese name itself was being etched into the very bones of Rome.

"It's magnificent," she murmured, her voice almost lost in the din.

"It will be," her mother, Silvia, replied, standing beside her. Silvia's eyes swept over the scene with a mix of pride and calculation. "When it's finished, it will be one of the greatest palaces in all of Italy, known as the Farnese palace. A testament to your father's vision."

"And his power," Costanza added softly, her gaze lingering on the towering scaffolds.

Silvia glanced at her daughter, a faint smile playing on her lips. "Power and vision often go hand in hand, my dear. Never forget that."

Alessandro approached them, his expression unreadable but his stride purposeful. "What do you think?" he asked, gesturing to the rising walls around them.

Costanza hesitated, searching for the right words. "It's… immense," she said finally. "And beautiful, even now."

Alessandro's lips curved into a faint smile. "Good. It should be both. A palace is not merely a home; it is a statement. This will be the seat of our family's power, a symbol of the Farnese legacy."

"Will it be finished in our lifetime?" Costanza asked, her tone carrying a hint of teasing.

Her father chuckled, the sound rare but genuine. "Rome was not built in a day, and neither will this palace. But it will endure, long after we are gone. That is what matters."

Costanza nodded, though her thoughts churned with questions. She admired her father's determination, but the scale of his ambition often felt overwhelming. Did he ever wonder if it was too much? Did he ever question what it might cost them all?

As they moved closer to the construction site, the full scope of the work became clear. Teams of laborers hauled massive blocks of travertine, their muscles straining under the weight. Architects poured over blueprints, their gestures animated as they debated the finer points of design. Sculptors worked meticulously on ornamental details, their hands steady despite the noise and dust around them.

Costanza paused to watch one of the sculptors at work. The man was shaping an intricate floral motif, the delicate curves emerging slowly from the unyielding stone. "It's incredible," she said softly.

The sculptor glanced up, offering a polite nod. "Thank you, my lady. Every detail must be perfect. The cardinal insists."

She smiled faintly. "Of course he does."

As they walked further, Costanza's younger brothers joined them. Pier Luigi, now fourteen, was less interested in the intricacies of architecture than in the potential the palace offered for prestige. "It's going to be the grandest building in Rome," he said, his voice brimming with excitement. "They'll all know the Farnese name."

"They already know it," Ranuccio replied with a quiet confidence. "But this will make them remember it forever."

Costanza couldn't help but smile at her brothers' differing perspectives. Pier Luigi was all energy and ambition, eager to step into their father's shoes. Ranuccio, on the other hand, had the contemplative air of someone who understood the weight of legacy without being consumed by it.

"What do you think, Costanza?" Ranuccio asked, his dark eyes searching hers.

She took a moment to consider her answer. "I think it's a symbol of everything Father believes in. Power, beauty, endurance. It's remarkable."

"And necessary," Alessandro interjected, his voice firm. "Without symbols, without legacy, power fades. The Farnese name must stand for something, not just in our lifetime, but for generations to come."

Costanza met her father's gaze, a flicker of understanding passing between them. She saw in him the weight of responsibility, the unrelenting drive to secure their place in history. It was both inspiring and daunting.

As the sun began to dip below the horizon, casting the construction site in golden light, the workers paused to rest. The palace, still incomplete, seemed to glow with promise.

Costanza stood with her family, her thoughts drifting to the future.

One day, this place would be finished. Its halls would echo with voices, its walls adorned with art, its gardens filled with life. It would be a testament to her father's vision and their family's resilience. But would it also be a monument to the sacrifices they made? To the burdens they carried?

Costanza didn't know the answers yet. But as she stood there, watching the foundations of the Farnese Palace rise, she felt the pull of her family's legacy more strongly than ever.

"Come," Alessandro said, his voice breaking the quiet. "There is much more to see."

Costanza followed, her footsteps steady, her thoughts heavier than before. The palace was not just a building—it was a promise, a challenge, and a legacy. And it was hers to carry, whether she wanted to or not.

Chapter 14

The grand hall of the Farnese Palace sparkled with opulence, the glow of hundreds of candles flickering against gilded mirrors and polished marble floors. Crimson and gold banners—emblazoned with the Farnese crest—hung from arched windows that framed a breathtaking view of Rome, its streets bathed in moonlight. Tonight, the palace was alive with voices, music, and the rustle of silk as Rome's most influential figures gathered to witness a moment that symbolized both power and ambition.

Costanza Farnese stood at the top of the sweeping staircase, her hands clasped tightly over her emerald velvet gown. The dress was exquisite, a masterpiece embroidered with gold thread and adorned with glimmering pearls along the neckline. Her sleeves, slashed to reveal the delicate white silk beneath, brushed her gloved hands as she adjusted her posture. Her dark hair, braided and twisted into an intricate crown, was accented by a single gold pin shaped like a fleur-de-lis.

"Breathe, my dear," her mother, Silvia, whispered, adjusting the hem of Costanza's gown with care. Dressed in deep burgundy satin and adorned with understated jewels, Silvia was the very image of poised authority. "You are a Farnese. You needn't be perfect, but you must be gracious."

Costanza nodded, inhaling slowly. "I'll try."

"That's all we ask," Silvia replied with a faint smile. "Now, let us begin."

As they descended the staircase, the hum of laughter and conversation swelled, mingling with the delicate strains of violins that filled the hall. All eyes turned toward them, curiosity and admiration lighting up the faces of the gathered nobles and dignitaries. At the far end of the room, Alessandro Farnese stood near a grand marble arch, his crimson cardinal's robes a vivid contrast to the golden hues around him. His commanding presence seemed to anchor the gathering, his expression calm but sharp.

Raising a hand, Alessandro quieted the room with ease. His voice carried effortlessly, filling the hall. "Friends, allies, esteemed guests," he began, his words laced with warmth and authority. "It is my honor to welcome you to the Farnese Palace, a home that stands as a testament to our shared history, faith, and future."

He paused, his gaze settling briefly on Costanza with a flicker of pride. "Tonight, we celebrate those bonds and the paths ahead. My daughter, Costanza, joins us this evening as a symbol of that future. Together, we look forward to strengthening our ties, in family, in friendship, and in faith. Please, enjoy the evening."

Polite applause rippled through the hall, and Costanza descended the final steps, her heart pounding in time with the music. She curtsied gracefully, the years of lessons guiding her movements even as nerves simmered beneath the surface.

The evening unfolded in a whirlwind of introductions, dances, and whispered conversations. Costanza moved through the crowd with practiced ease, her every word measured and her every step deliberate. Around her, women's gowns shimmered with vibrant brocades and embroidered silks, their jewels catching the warm candlelight. The men, dressed in doublets adorned with intricate patterns and velvet capes, exuded confidence and intrigue.

"The Farnese girl is stunning," Costanza overheard one woman whisper behind her fan. "Alessandro has outdone himself tonight."

Another voice, low and calculating, added, "Sforza will be pleased. She carries herself well—graceful, but not overly timid."

At the center of the hall, couples swayed to the music, their movements elegant and deliberate. The scent of honeyed wine, roasted meats, and fresh roses filled the air, mingling with the faint notes of the violins and lutes. Costanza's dance card filled quickly, and one by one, suitors took her onto the polished floor, eager to secure her attention, if only for a moment.

Among them was a young nobleman with striking blue eyes and a self-assured smile. "Giulio Orsini," he introduced himself with a bow as they stepped into a stately pavane. "A pleasure to finally meet you, Lady Costanza."

She inclined her head slightly, her hazel eyes steady. "The pleasure is mine, Signor Orsini. And what brings you here tonight?"

"Admiration for your father, of course," he replied smoothly. "And curiosity about the Farnese heir I've heard so much about."

Costanza raised an eyebrow, a flicker of amusement crossing her face. "And what have you heard?"

"That you are intelligent and... strong-willed," Giulio said with a grin. "Qualities I find quite admirable."

"And rare in women?" she teased, a hint of sharpness in her tone.

"Rare," he admitted, "But not unwelcome. Beauty fades if it stands alone, but wit endures."

Her lips curved into a faint smile. "A bold sentiment, Signor Orsini. I'll remember it."

As the evening stretched on, Costanza found her way onto the terrace, the cool night air a welcome reprieve from the heat of the crowded ballroom. She leaned against the marble balustrade, her gaze drifting over the lights of Rome, their soft glow a tapestry of ambition and history.

"You slipped away," a familiar voice said behind her.

She turned to see Pier Luigi, dressed in ceremonial finery that made him look older than his fourteen years. He leaned casually against the railing, his usual mischievous grin softened by genuine admiration. "You're handling this well," he said. "Better than I would."

Costanza chuckled softly. "Thank you. But it's... overwhelming."

Pier Luigi nodded, his expression growing serious. "It always is. But you're Farnese. You'll manage."

She studied her younger brother, sensing the pressure he bore even at his young age. "And you? Are you ready for your role?"

He shrugged, the weight of their family's expectations shadowing his confidence. "I'll have to be, won't I? Just like you."

They stood in silence for a moment, the bond between them unspoken but palpable. Finally, Costanza straightened, her shoulders squaring as she pushed away her own doubts. "Well," she said with renewed resolve, "We'd better not keep them waiting."

Pier Luigi offered his arm, a rare gesture of camaraderie. Together, they returned to the ballroom, their steps purposeful as they faced the world that awaited them.

Chapter 15

The Farnese Palace buzzed with life as the evening wore on, the grand event unfolding into whispered intrigue and subtle power plays. Costanza had just stepped away from the dance floor, her feet aching from hours of graceful pivots and poised curtsies. She found herself near one of the ornate columns lining the ballroom, momentarily hidden from view by the flowing crimson drapes.

As she reached for a goblet of wine from a passing servant, she caught a familiar voice—Giulio Orsini. His tone, light and teasing earlier in their dance, had grown louder, rougher. Curious, Costanza turned her head slightly, the folds of the drapery concealing her presence.

"I'm saying she's striking, yes," Giulio said, his words clipped, "But a cardinal's bastard doesn't make her marriage material for a house like yours."

The words struck Costanza like a blow, her breath catching in her throat. She peeked around the drape and saw Giulio standing near the carved marble fireplace, his posture relaxed, but his words barbed. Opposite him stood a man she had not yet been officially introduced to—tall, broad-shouldered, and dressed in a rich black doublet with gold accents. His expression was calm, but his dark eyes betrayed a sharp intensity.

"You overstep," the man said evenly, though there was an edge to his voice. "Lady Costanza's name carries more than enough weight to stand beside mine."

Giulio smirked, lifting his goblet as if in a mock salute. "Oh, come now, Bosio. We're friends, aren't we? I meant no harm. But let's not pretend this is purely about politics. Surely you've considered—"

"Enough," Bosio Sforza interrupted, his tone firm. He took a step closer to Giulio, his presence commanding. "Lady Costanza is not to be spoken of so carelessly, nor in my presence."

Giulio's smile faltered, but he held his ground. "No offense, of course," he said, his voice losing some of its earlier confidence. "You know how these things are."

Bosio's gaze didn't waver. "What I know is that you would do well to remember the Farnese name. And her father's reach."

For a moment, the tension crackled like the fire in the hearth behind them. Then Giulio gave a curt nod, muttering something Costanza couldn't catch before retreating into the crowd.

Costanza let the drape fall back into place and stepped away from her hidden vantage point. Her pulse was racing, her emotions a whirlwind of indignation and curiosity. Who was this Bosio Sforza, and why had he come to her defense so swiftly?

Amid the swirl of color and motion in the crowded ballroom, her gaze fell on the man who had spoken in her defense. He was taller than many around him, his frame broad-shouldered and commanding without being imposing. His dark hair, streaked lightly with silver at the temples, framed a face etched with lines that hinted at both experience and the weight of responsibility. His sharp jawline and aquiline nose lent him an air of authority, softened only by his warm, dark eyes—eyes that seemed to hold secrets and stories he had yet to share.

His attire was impeccable, a black doublet adorned with subtle gold embroidery that caught the flicker of the candlelight. The understated elegance of his clothing, paired with his deliberate movements, suggested a man who understood the balance between confidence and restraint. There was no flourish for attention, no unnecessary gesture; he simply existed, solid and unshakable, like the foundations of a fortress.

Yet it was not merely his appearance that caught Costanza's attention—it was his presence. He carried himself with a quiet gravity, the kind of man who commanded respect without needing to demand it. She felt an odd pull, equal parts curiosity and caution. He was unlike anyone she had danced with or spoken to that evening, a figure who seemed at once part of the world she inhabited and somehow removed from its frivolities.

Her thoughts were interrupted when the man himself appeared from the crowd.

He approached with purposeful steps, his dark eyes locking onto hers as if he had known she was there all along. When he stopped before her, he bowed slightly, his expression softening.

"Lady Costanza," he said, his voice steady and rich. "I hope I did not startle you."

Costanza straightened, drawing herself to her full height. "Not at all," she replied, though her voice carried a hint of caution. "You seem to know my name, yet I have not had the pleasure of yours."

He smiled faintly, the corners of his mouth lifting just enough to soften his otherwise serious demeanor. "Bosio Sforza, at your service."

The name finally struck her. This was the man her father had spoken of, the suitor whose name had been whispered in countless conversations. She studied him for a moment, noting the confidence in his posture, the strength in his hands, and the measured calm of his expression.

"It seems I owe you my thanks, Signor Sforza," she said. "Though I am curious—why defend my honor so quickly?"

He tilted his head slightly, his gaze unwavering. "Because it was the right thing to do. And because no one—especially not Orsini—should speak ill of someone who carries the Farnese name."

Her lips pressed into a thin line, her mind racing. "You speak as though you already know me."

"I know of you," he corrected gently. "And tonight, I see that the stories were not exaggerated. You are as poised and intelligent as they said."

Costanza felt a flush rise to her cheeks but quickly masked it with a small smile. "Stories have a way of embellishing the truth."

"Perhaps," Bosio replied, his tone warm but firm. "But some truths do not need embellishment."

The weight of his words hung between them for a moment before he offered his arm. "Shall we rejoin the festivities? It would be an honor to accompany you."

Costanza hesitated only briefly before placing her hand on his arm. "Very well," she said, her voice steady despite the flutter of nerves in her chest.

As they stepped into the light of the grand ballroom, Costanza couldn't help but glance up at him. There was something different about Bosio Sforza—an air of strength and conviction that both unsettled and intrigued her. Tonight, the palace had been a stage for many things: alliances, whispers, and power plays. But in this moment, as she walked beside him, it felt like the beginning of something else entirely.

Chapter 16

The air in the grand ballroom had shifted. What had begun as a dazzling display of wealth and influence now carried an undercurrent of tension, rippling through the crowd like the faintest vibration of a plucked string. Costanza Farnese, standing near the terrace, felt it keenly. Her evening had been a whirlwind of introductions and dances, of polite smiles and measured words. But now, something else hung in the air, intangible yet undeniable.

Her gaze inevitably found Bosio Sforza, standing with her father near the edge of the hall. Alessandro's expression was measured, his words deliberate, but it was Bosio's quiet intensity that held her attention. He stood as though he belonged, his commanding presence requiring no announcement. Earlier, his swift defense of her had stirred something within her—something she couldn't quite name. Did he act out of duty, a calculated move to align himself with her family? Or had it meant something more?

Her thoughts were interrupted by the sharp ring of laughter cutting through the hum of the crowd. Turning toward the sound, she caught sight of Giulio Orsini, his face flushed with wine, gesturing animatedly toward a small group of nobles. The amused smirks and awkward glances of his companions suggested trouble brewing.

"Let's not pretend," Giulio's voice rose, dripping with mockery. "That the Farnese name is untouchable. Ambition built on secrets is a fragile thing, no matter how grand the palace."

The room fell silent, the murmurs fading as his words hung heavy in the air. Costanza's chest tightened, her hands gripping the folds of her gown. She could feel the weight of dozens of eyes darting between her and Giulio, their gazes expectant, waiting for someone to act.

Before she could step forward, another voice cut through the tension, calm but laced with steel. "Careful, Orsini," Bosio Sforza said, his deep tone carrying effortlessly across the room. "You speak boldly for a man whose own family's fortunes rest on borrowed favor."

Giulio turned, his smug grin faltering as he met Bosio's steady gaze. "Oh, come now, Sforza," he said, his bravado wavering slightly. "Surely even you can see the irony."

"What I see," Bosio replied, taking a deliberate step closer, "Is a man who enjoys testing the patience of those more disciplined than himself. Tonight is not the time for petty insults or drunken indiscretions. If you have something to say about the Farnese name, perhaps you should bring it to Cardinal Alessandro directly." His tone darkened, each word deliberate. "Unless, of course, you lack the courage."

The room seemed to hold its breath, the tension crackling like a spark waiting to ignite. Giulio's face reddened, his smirk replaced with a scowl. After a long pause, he muttered something unintelligible and turned on his heel, retreating into the crowd with his entourage trailing behind.

The crowd shifted back into movement, the lull of whispers slowly rebuilding. Costanza, her heart still racing, slipped out to the terrace. The cool night air brushed against her flushed cheeks, a welcome reprieve from the stifling weight of the ballroom. She leaned against the marble balustrade, her gaze falling on the distant lights of Rome glittering like stars on earth.

Her thoughts churned. She had expected many things tonight—conversations of alliances, dances with potential suitors—but not Giulio's crude insult. Nor had she expected Bosio's decisive intervention. His words had been sharp, calculated, but there was something in his tone that unsettled her. Something she couldn't place.

"Costanza," a familiar voice called gently behind her.

She turned quickly, her breath catching as Bosio Sforza stepped into view. His calm presence, so steady and assured, sent a ripple through the turmoil in her chest. He stopped a few paces away, his hands clasped behind his back, his expression soft yet unreadable.

"You shouldn't let Orsini's words trouble you," he said, his voice low. "Men like him thrive on provocation. They're easily forgotten."

"I'm not troubled by him," Costanza replied, though her tone betrayed the lingering tension. "It's the way everyone looks at me—as though I'm not a person but a prize to be won, or a pawn to be moved."

Bosio's brow furrowed, and he stepped closer, his dark eyes searching hers. "You are far more than a pawn, Costanza. Anyone who fails to see that is blind."

Her breath caught at his words, her pulse quickening. "Why did you defend me tonight?" she asked, her voice softening. "Was it for politics, or something else?"

Bosio hesitated, his gaze steady but unreadable. "As I said before, I defended you because it was right," he said carefully. "But also because I see something in you that deserves defending."

The sincerity in his voice disarmed her, leaving her unsure of what to say. Gratitude mixed with confusion, a flicker of warmth stirring in a way that both intrigued and unsettled her.

"And what is that?" she asked, her voice barely above a whisper.

"Strength," he said simply. "Even when you doubt yourself, it's there. Don't let anyone take that from you."

Costanza looked away, her cheeks warming under his steady gaze. "I don't know if I'm as strong as you think."

"You are," Bosio replied, his tone firm yet kind. "And one day, you'll see it too."

As Bosio bowed slightly and returned to the ballroom, Costanza remained on the terrace, her thoughts tangled. The evening, meant to be a celebration of her family's power, had become something far more personal. Giulio's insult, Bosio's defense, and the emotions now swirling within her—none of it felt simple.

She glanced toward the stars, their distant light as steadfast as the man who had just left her. She wondered if he had meant his words, if there was more to him than the alliances and strategies that defined her world. And why, she thought, did she feel so desperate to know?

With a deep breath, she straightened her shoulders and turned back toward the grand hall. Whatever the answers, tonight had changed something in her. And though she didn't yet know what, she felt certain it would follow her long after the music had faded.

Chapter 17

The sunlight filtered through the high arched windows of the Ruffini villa, casting soft patterns on the marble floors. The early morning air carried the scent of dew from the garden outside, mingling with the faint aroma of freshly baked bread wafting from the kitchens. Yet, despite the tranquility of her surroundings, Costanza Farnese could not still her restless thoughts.

She sat by the window in her chambers, her hands idle in her lap. The embroidery hoop before her lay forgotten, the delicate silk thread half-pulled through a rose petal she had begun the day before. Her gaze drifted over the rolling hills of the Roman countryside, but her mind was far from the quiet beauty of the landscape.

Bosio Sforza.

His name lingered in her thoughts like the faint echo of a melody, refusing to fade. The memory of his voice, steady and unwavering, still resonated within her. The way he had defended her against Giulio Orsini's cruel words had stirred something deep inside her—a mix of gratitude, curiosity, and something else she couldn't quite name.

"You are far more than a pawn, Costanza."

The words played over and over in her mind, a gentle challenge and an unexpected comfort. Was it sincerity that she had heard in his voice? Or was it calculated, another move in the intricate game of alliances that governed their lives? She had grown accustomed to reading the motives behind others' actions, yet with Bosio, she felt unsure.

"Costanza?" Her mother's voice broke the silence, drawing her attention. Silvia Ruffini stood in the doorway, her expression both warm and observant. Dressed in a flowing gown of deep lavender, she carried herself with the quiet authority of someone who had navigated these waters before.

"Yes, Mother?" Costanza replied, straightening in her seat.

Silvia stepped into the room, her gaze flicking briefly to the untouched embroidery before returning to her daughter. "You've been distant all morning. Your mind seems far from home."

Costanza hesitated, then offered a small smile. "I suppose I'm still tired from last night."

"Hmm," Silvia said, her tone carrying a note of disbelief. She crossed the room and sat beside Costanza, resting a gentle hand on her daughter's arm. "It wouldn't have anything to do with Bosio Sforza, would it?"

The question caught Costanza off guard, and a faint blush rose to her cheeks. "Why would you think that?"

"Because I saw the way he looked at you," Silvia said, her voice soft but knowing. "And the way you looked at him."

Costanza dropped her gaze to her hands, her fingers twisting the edge of her gown. "He defended me," she admitted. "When Giulio Orsini spoke against our family. But I don't understand why. Was it duty? Politics? Or something else?"

Silvia smiled faintly. "Perhaps it was all of those things. Or perhaps it was simply because he saw you for who you are."

"And who is that?" Costanza asked, her voice tinged with doubt. "To most of the world, I'm just a tool for Father's ambitions."

"To the world, perhaps," Silvia replied, her tone firm. "But to those who matter, you are far more. Bosio may have seen that. Or he may simply be a man who values honor. Either way, the question is not what he thinks of you, Costanza. The question is what you think of him."

Silvia's words stayed with her long after her mother had left the room. What did she think of Bosio Sforza? She had admired his composure, his ability to command respect without raising his voice. She had been struck by the warmth in his dark eyes, the sincerity in his tone. And yet, she couldn't shake the nagging fear that it was all part of some greater strategy.

Costanza rose from her seat and moved to the window, resting her hands on the sill. The sunlight warmed her skin, but her thoughts remained clouded. The life she led was one of careful calculation, of playing roles and fulfilling expectations. Could she allow herself to believe in something—someone—that might be genuine?

Her gaze drifted to the garden below, where the roses bloomed in wild abundance. The beauty of the scene brought a rare moment of clarity. Whatever Bosio's reasons, his words had touched something within her. He had seen her not as a pawn, but as a person. And for that alone, she couldn't stop thinking of him.

The sound of footsteps in the corridor broke her reverie. A servant appeared in the doorway, bowing politely. "My lady," he said, holding out a folded piece of parchment sealed with crimson wax. "A letter has arrived for you."

Costanza's heart quickened as she took the letter, her fingers trembling slightly as she broke the seal. The handwriting was bold and precise, the words direct:

Lady Costanza,
I hope this letter finds you well. Though I spoke
little last night, there is much I wished to say.
Your strength and grace did not go unnoticed. I
hope, in time, we might speak again under
calmer circumstances. Until then, know that you
are thought of with the highest regard.
Yours,
Bosio Sforza.

Her breath caught as she read the words, her heart racing. She folded the letter carefully, holding it close as she leaned against the window. The sun seemed brighter now, the roses below more vibrant. For the first time, she allowed herself to smile—a small, hesitant smile, but one filled with the promise of something more.

Chapter 18

Costanza paced the length of her chambers, her thoughts restless despite the calm morning light spilling through the windows. The letter from Bosio Sforza lay folded on her writing desk, its carefully chosen words replaying in her mind. She couldn't ignore the growing pull she felt toward the man, yet so much about him remained a mystery.

"Maria," Costanza called, her voice steady but tinged with determination.

Her maidservant appeared in the doorway moments later, her hands folded neatly in front of her apron. "Yes, my lady?"

Costanza hesitated, smoothing the folds of her gown as though the act might organize her swirling thoughts. "I need your help. Discreetly."

Maria nodded, her expression calm but curious. "Of course, my lady. What would you have me do?"

"I want to know more about Bosio Sforza," Costanza said, her voice softening slightly as if the mere mention of his name made her vulnerable. "Where he comes from, who he is. Anything you can find."

Maria's brows lifted slightly, though she quickly schooled her features. "I will see what I can learn," she said with a small bow. "Give me a day, my lady."

Costanza gave a faint smile of gratitude, though her stomach churned with unease. She wasn't sure what she hoped to discover, but she knew she couldn't move forward until she understood the man who had so unexpectedly unsettled her heart.

The next evening, Maria returned, her expression careful as she stepped into Costanza's chambers. In her hands, she held a folded piece of parchment with her own notes.

"My lady," she began, "I've spoken to those who know of Signor Sforza, both here in Rome and beyond. I believe you'll find this information of interest."

Costanza gestured for her to sit, her curiosity outweighing any decorum. "Tell me everything," she said.

Maria unfolded the parchment, scanning her notes briefly before beginning. "Bosio Sforza is the head of the Sforza family branch from Santafiora, a powerful lineage tied to the Duchy of Milan. Though not the direct heirs to the duchy, his family has maintained considerable influence in both politics and commerce."

Costanza nodded, her fingers curling slightly against her lap. "And his reputation?"

Maria hesitated. "He is widely regarded as a man of integrity, though some say he can be… cold. Practical. His loyalties are strong, but they are earned, not given lightly."

"Has he ever been married?" Costanza asked, her voice quieter now.

"No, my lady. Though there have been rumors of arrangements in the past, none came to fruition. He is said to value strength and intellect in a partner, which has made him more selective than most men of his rank."

Costanza felt a faint blush rise to her cheeks but quickly masked it with a thoughtful nod. "And his role in Rome?"

"Signor Sforza has recently been involved in negotiations with the Church, likely on matters of land and influence," Maria said. "He has the ear of powerful men, but he does not flaunt it. Many see him as a man of strategy—a chess player who considers every move carefully."

Costanza leaned back, her mind racing. The picture Maria painted was of a man both formidable and principled, someone who navigated the intricate web of politics with precision. Yet it did little to explain the warmth she had seen in his eyes or the sincerity in his words.

"Is there more?" she asked, sensing that Maria was holding something back.

The maid hesitated, then nodded. "One of the servants at last night's event mentioned seeing Signor Sforza speak with Cardinal Alessandro after the ballroom had emptied. Though I could not confirm what was said, the conversation seemed... pointed."

Costanza's stomach tightened. "Pointed how?"

"From what I gathered, your father and Signor Sforza spoke of alliances. Some believe that the defense of your honor last night may not have been entirely spontaneous."

The words struck a nerve, though Costanza tried to hide her disappointment. She had suspected as much—that Bosio's actions might have been tied to politics rather than genuine care. But hearing it spoken aloud felt like a blow nonetheless.

"Thank you, Maria," she said quietly. "That will be all."

The maid bowed and left the room, leaving Costanza alone with her thoughts.

~

Elsewhere in Rome, Bosio Sforza sat in his study, his brow furrowed as he reviewed the correspondence from the previous day. Letters from his advisors, landholders, and even the Vatican crowded his desk, each demanding his attention. Yet his thoughts kept drifting back to the Farnese Palace, to the woman whose sharp gaze and quiet strength had lingered in his mind long after the music had faded.

Costanza Farnese.

He had seen many women like her—noble daughters raised to embody grace and duty, their lives dictated by alliances and expectations. Yet, there was something different about Costanza. Beneath the poise and refinement, he sensed a spark of defiance, a hunger for more than the role the world had assigned her.

He leaned back in his chair, his fingers steepled as he considered his next move. The conversation with Cardinal Alessandro had been brief but clear: the Farnese patriarch saw the value in a union between their families. The idea was not unwelcome—Costanza was intelligent, composed, and undoubtedly beautiful. But Bosio was not a man to be swayed by appearances alone.

He thought of her standing on the terrace, her expression conflicted as she spoke of feeling like a pawn in someone else's game. He had seen her vulnerability then, but also her strength—the quiet determination that would serve her well in a world that rarely valued such qualities in women.

His decision was made, though it was not without risk. Aligning himself with the Farnese family could bolster his influence, but it could also entangle him in their complexities. Still, he found himself drawn to Costanza in a way he hadn't expected. Whether it was strategy or something deeper, he couldn't yet say.

Bosio dipped his pen into the inkwell and began to write, his bold script filling the page with precision. Lady Costanza deserved more than silence.

Chapter 19

The summer brought a sweltering heat to Rome, the kind that lingered in the air and clung to the marble walls of the Ruffini villa. Yet the Farnese family bustled with activity. Costanza Farnese stood on the cusp of a moment that would shape her future. That evening, the Sforza family was coming, and she knew why. The years of careful negotiation, whispers of alliances, and familial duty had led to this night—her formal engagement to Bosio II Sforza.

The carriage bearing Bosio Sforza and his entourage arrived at dusk, its wheels crunching over the gravel drive. The Sforza crest, emblazoned on the side, gleamed in the golden light. Bosio stepped out first. Dressed in a tailored doublet of black velvet with gold accents, he exuded the confidence of a man accustomed to commanding attention.

Costanza stood beside her mother, Silvia Ruffini, her hands clasped tightly before her to hide her nerves. She wore a gown of deep sapphire blue, its rich fabric a nod to her father's cardinal robes. Her hair, arranged in an elegant twist, framed her youthful but resolute face.

When Bosio entered the villa, he greeted Cardinal Alessandro Farnese with a slight bow, their exchange warm but laced with the undertones of strategy.

"Welcome, Bosio," Alessandro said, his voice steady. "It is a pleasure to see you again."

"And an honor to be here, Cardinal," Bosio replied, his gaze flickering briefly to Costanza. His expression, though measured, carried a hint of curiosity.

The dinner that followed was a masterpiece of Renaissance opulence. The long table, adorned with candelabras and floral arrangements, groaned under the weight of roasted meats, fresh bread, and ripe fruit. The conversation among the men flowed easily, touching on matters of state, the shifting allegiances within Italy, and the Pope's latest decrees.

Costanza, seated across from Bosio, spoke only when addressed. Her replies were poised, her voice calm, though her heart raced whenever her future husband's gaze met hers. She studied him discreetly throughout the meal, noting the lines etched into his face, the silver streaking his dark hair, and the way he spoke with quiet authority.

It wasn't until the final course had been cleared that Alessandro rose, his commanding presence silencing the room.

"Friends," he began, his voice carrying over the gathered guests, "Tonight marks the beginning of a union that will strengthen not only our families but the bonds that tie Rome and Tuscany together. My daughter, Costanza, has come of age, and it is with great pride that I announce her engagement to Bosio Sforza."

Polite applause followed, though Costanza felt as though the world had stilled around her. Bosio's eyes found hers, and he gave her a slight, reassuring nod.

Later, as the evening wore on and the guests lingered over their wine, Bosio approached Costanza. His steps were purposeful but not hurried, his presence steady and calm.

"Lady Costanza," he said, bowing slightly. "May I have a moment of your time?"

"Of course," she replied, heart racing, rising gracefully from her seat.

He led her to the villa's garden, where the cool night air carried the scent of blooming jasmine. The moonlight bathed the paths in silver, lending a dreamlike quality to the scene. For a moment, they walked in silence, the only sound the soft rustling of leaves.

"I imagine this evening must feel overwhelming," Bosio said at last, his voice warm but measured.

"It does," Costanza admitted. "But I have long understood that this day would come."

He glanced at her, a faint smile curving his lips. "You speak with the composure of someone far older than seventeen. Your father has every reason to be proud."

She hesitated before speaking again, her voice quieter. "And you, Signor Sforza? Are you pleased with this arrangement?"

He stopped walking, turning to face her fully. "I am," he said simply. "Not because of politics or alliances, though those things matter. But because I see in you a strength and grace that will carry you far. This is no small decision for either of us, but I believe it is the right one."

His candor disarmed her, and for a moment, she allowed herself to truly look at him—not as a stranger or a suitor, but as the man who would soon be her husband. "I hope I can meet your expectations," she said, her voice steady despite the flutter in her chest.

"And I hope to meet yours," Bosio replied. He extended his hand, palm up. "Shall we return?"

She placed her hand lightly in his, the warmth of his touch grounding her. "Yes," she said softly. "Let's."

The next morning, the engagement was formalized with a signed agreement between the Farnese and Sforza families. The document detailed the dowry, the expectations of both parties, and the promise of mutual support between their houses.

For Costanza, the act was both monumental and surreal. As she watched her father sign the parchment with a flourish, she felt the weight of her new reality settle over her. She was no longer just a daughter of the Farnese family; she was now a link between two powerful houses, a symbol of alliance and ambition.

Bosio, standing beside her, leaned in slightly as the ink dried. "We will make this work, Lady Costanza," he said quietly. "Together."

She glanced up at him, finding reassurance in his steady gaze. "Yes," she replied, her resolve firming. "We will."

Chapter 20

The weeks following Costanza Farnese's engagement to Bosio Sforza were a blur of preparation and ceremony. Both families moved swiftly to ensure their alliance was cemented with all the pomp and circumstance befitting their noble stations. Yet beneath the surface of this seemingly harmonious union, tensions simmered.

It was a stormy evening when a messenger arrived at the Farnese villa, his cloak soaked through and his face pale from the rain. Pier Luigi, now fifteen and ever curious, intercepted the man and brought him to Cardinal Alessandro Farnese's study. Costanza, wandering the halls, caught a glimpse of the commotion and lingered near the door, her curiosity piqued.

Inside the study, Alessandro unfolded the letter the messenger had brought, his sharp eyes scanning the page. As he read, his expression darkened, and he slammed a hand onto the desk.

"This cannot stand," he said, his voice low and taut with anger.

"What is it, Father?" Pier Luigi asked, stepping forward.

Alessandro hesitated, his gaze darting to the messenger before speaking. "There are rumors—accusations—that Bosio's loyalty to Rome may not be as steadfast as it seems."

Pier Luigi frowned. "Accusations of what kind?"

"Correspondence with Florence," Alessandro said. "Unverified, but if true, it would be a betrayal of the highest order. The Medici cannot be trusted, and Florence is too closely tied to French interests."

Costanza, still hidden in the hallway, felt her stomach twist. She had barely begun to reconcile herself to her engagement, and now this shadow threatened to unravel everything.

That evening, the family gathered in the villa's drawing room. Alessandro, seated at the head of the room, relayed the news to Silvia, Pier Luigi, and Ranuccio. Costanza sat quietly to the side, her hands clasped tightly in her lap.

"Do we believe it?" Silvia asked, her tone calm but her eyes sharp.

"We cannot ignore it," Alessandro replied. "If Bosio has been in communication with Florence, it calls into question his intentions for this alliance."

Pier Luigi's face hardened. "Then we confront him. If he's deceived us, he must answer for it."

"And what if the rumors are false?" Costanza said, her voice cutting through the tension. All eyes turned to her, but she held her ground. "What if this is a ploy to sow discord between our families? Breaking the engagement over unproven accusations would harm us as much as it would harm him."

Her father's gaze softened slightly. "You are wise to consider that, Costanza. But this is not merely about rumors. Politics is rarely so simple."

The next day, Bosio Sforza arrived at the villa, summoned by Alessandro under the guise of discussing wedding preparations. Costanza watched from an upper balcony as his carriage approached. His expression, as always, was composed, but there was a tension in his posture she had not noticed before.

When he entered Alessandro's study, the air seemed to crackle with unspoken words. Costanza found herself slipping into the hallway again, her heart pounding as she pressed herself against the wall to listen.

"Bosio," Alessandro began, his tone even but cool, "I have heard troubling reports. They suggest you have been in communication with Florence. Is this true?"

There was a pause before Bosio replied, his voice calm but firm. "I will not deny that I have corresponded with Florence, but it is not as you think. My interests are in securing peace for my holdings in Santa Fiora, which lie dangerously close to Medici territory. I have no intention of betraying this alliance."

"And yet," Alessandro said, his tone sharpening, "The Medici are no friends of Rome. Any dealings with them place this union in jeopardy."

Bosio stepped closer to the desk, his voice rising slightly. "Do you think me a fool, Cardinal? I know what is at stake. My loyalty to Rome and this family remains unshaken, but I will not endanger my people by ignoring the reality of Florence's proximity. This is not betrayal; it is pragmatism."

Unable to remain silent any longer, Costanza stepped into the room. Both men turned to her, their surprise evident, but she kept her head high.

"Father," she said, her voice steady despite the pounding of her heart, "Bosio has always acted with honor. You taught me that alliances require trust. If we doubt him now, we undermine everything this union was meant to build."

Alessandro's eyes narrowed, but he said nothing, his gaze flickering between his daughter and Bosio.

Bosio's expression softened slightly as he looked at her. "Lady Costanza speaks the truth," he said. "I have no love for Florence or the Medici, but I will not see my people suffer because of Rome's enmity. If this is a cause for concern, then I ask you to trust in the strength of our alliance to overcome it."

The room fell silent as Alessandro weighed his options. Finally, he rose from his chair, his expression unreadable.

"Very well," he said. "We will proceed with the engagement. But know this, Bosio—any hint of disloyalty, and the consequences will be swift."

Bosio inclined his head. "Understood."

As he left the study, Costanza followed him into the corridor. "Thank you," she said softly. "For being honest."

Bosio turned to her, his dark eyes unreadable. "Trust is not easily earned, Lady Costanza. But I hope I have done enough to keep yours."

"You have," she replied, though her heart was still heavy with doubt.

Though the engagement remained intact, the rumors cast a shadow over the alliance. Costanza felt the strain in every conversation, the unspoken tension that lingered between her father and Bosio. Yet she also felt a growing respect for the man she was to marry—a man willing to defend his people, even at the risk of suspicion.

As the days passed, Costanza resolved to prove herself worthy of the role she was to play. She would bridge the divide between her family and Bosio's, not through politics or power, but through the loyalty and trust she so deeply valued.

But even as she made this vow, she couldn't shake the feeling that this was only the beginning of the challenges they would face together.

Chapter 21

The wedding of Costanza Farnese and Bosio II Sforza promised to be one of the most lavish events of the year. With the union of two powerful families, every detail carried the weight of political significance and social prestige. The weeks leading up to the ceremony transformed both the Farnese villa and the chosen venue into hives of activity, where seamstresses, cooks, and artisans worked tirelessly to meet the lofty expectations set by Cardinal Alessandro Farnese.

It was decided that the wedding would be held in Santa Maria Sopra Minerva, a grand Dominican church nestled in the heart of Rome. Renowned for its Gothic architecture and its proximity to the Vatican, the church symbolized the sanctity of the union and the Farnese family's deep ties to the Papacy.

The church's interior, with its soaring vaulted ceilings and intricate frescoes, provided the perfect backdrop for the ceremony. Cardinal Farnese ensured that additional decorations—garlands of flowers, gilded candlesticks, and tapestries bearing the crests of the Farnese and Sforza families—would transform the already opulent space into a vision of divine beauty.

Costanza's wedding gown was the talk of the household. Commissioned from one of the finest ateliers in Rome, the gown was crafted from cream-colored silk, its bodice embroidered with delicate golden vines and pearls. A long veil of fine lace, imported from Venice, was to complete the ensemble, held in place by a jeweled tiara gifted by Silvia Ruffini, Costanza's mother.

During a fitting, Costanza stood still as the seamstresses bustled around her, adjusting the gown's hem and perfecting every detail. Her reflection in the tall mirror showed a young woman poised and elegant, though the weight of the occasion lingered in her expression.

"You look beautiful," Silvia said softly, placing a reassuring hand on her daughter's shoulder.

"Thank you, Mother," Costanza replied, though her voice carried a hint of apprehension. "It all feels so... overwhelming."

"It should," Silvia said with a small smile. "This is not just a wedding; it is the start of a new chapter for our family. But you are ready for this."

The guest list read like a who's who of Renaissance Rome. Cardinals, noble families, and even ambassadors from Spain and Venice were invited. Pope Leo X himself was rumored to make an appearance, though whether he would officiate or merely observe remained uncertain.

For days, couriers came and went from the villa, delivering invitations embossed with the Farnese and Sforza crests. Every acceptance added to the pressure of ensuring the wedding was a flawless display of the families' wealth and influence.

Following the ceremony, the reception was to be held at the Farnese palace, where the gardens were transformed into a scene from a mythological painting. Long tables draped in crimson and gold were set beneath canopies of ivy and flowers. A fountain, adorned with newly sculpted cherubs, served as the centerpiece, surrounded by trays of the finest fruits, pastries, and wines.

Chefs from Tuscany and Rome collaborated to create a feast worthy of the occasion, with dishes ranging from roasted pheasants and honey-glazed boar to delicate tarts and marzipan shaped like flowers. Every detail, from the arrangement of the dishes to the serving of the wines, was rehearsed to perfection.

In the days leading up to the wedding, Pier Luigi Farnese took it upon himself to oversee certain aspects of the preparations. He spent hours in the gardens, ensuring the decorations met his father's exacting standards. Despite his occasional complaints about the monotony of the task, it was clear that Pier Luigi took pride in his role.

"You're ensuring perfection, brother," Costanza said one afternoon as she joined him by the fountain. "Father couldn't have chosen anyone better."

Pier Luigi smirked, wiping his hands on his tunic. "Don't flatter me too much, or I'll start expecting rewards for all this work."

They laughed together, a moment of levity amidst the whirlwind of preparations.

On the eve of the wedding, a gift arrived from Bosio Sforza: a gilded mirror framed with delicate carvings of roses and ivy. Accompanying it was a note in his hand:

"To my future wife,
May this mirror reflect not only your beauty but the strength and grace I have come to admire.
– Bosio"

Costanza traced her fingers over the engraving, her heart softening. The gesture, though simple, carried a sincerity that she hadn't expected. She placed the note carefully in her writing desk, reading it once more before tucking it away.

On the morning of the wedding, Costanza found herself alone in the villa's chapel, her hands clasped in prayer. The soft glow of the candles illuminated her serene features, though her heart raced with anticipation.

"Give me strength," she whispered. "To be the wife he needs, to fulfill my family's hopes, and to find peace in this new life."

The faint sound of footsteps interrupted her thoughts, and she turned to see Silvia standing in the doorway. "It's time, my dear," she said gently.

Costanza rose, smoothing her gown. "Then let's begin."

Chapter 22

The morning sun bathed Rome in a golden glow, its light cascading over the rooftops and church spires, bringing a rare serenity to the bustling city. At Santa Maria Sopra Minerva, preparations for the Farnese-Sforza wedding were already in full swing. The grand church, with its soaring arches and vibrant frescoes, stood ready to witness the union of two of Italy's most powerful families.

Inside the Farnese villa, the atmosphere was anything but serene. Servants rushed through the halls, carrying garments, arranging last-minute details, and attending to the bride. In her chambers, Costanza Farnese stood motionless as her mother, Silvia Ruffini, adjusted the final details of her gown.

"You look radiant," Silvia said softly, stepping back to admire her daughter. The gown, crafted from fine silk and adorned with gold embroidery, shimmered in the morning light. A delicate lace veil framed Costanza's face, her dark eyes reflecting a mixture of nerves and resolve.

"Thank you, Mother," Costanza replied, her voice steady despite the storm of emotions within her.

The bells of Santa Maria Sopra Minerva rang out as Costanza's carriage approached the church. Crowds of onlookers lined the streets, craning their necks to catch a glimpse of the bride. Inside, the guests—an assemblage of Rome's most influential figures—rose to their feet as she entered.

The church was a vision of opulence, its aisles lined with garlands of flowers and its altar adorned with gilded candelabras. Standing at the altar, Bosio Sforza turned as Costanza began her walk down the aisle, her arm linked with Cardinal Alessandro Farnese. His expression remained composed, but a flicker of something—admiration, perhaps—crossed his face as their eyes met.

Costanza's heart pounded with each step, the weight of expectation heavy on her shoulders. As she reached the altar, Alessandro placed her hand in Bosio's and stepped aside, his expression unreadable.

The ceremony proceeded with solemnity, the priest's voice echoing through the vaulted chamber as he spoke of the sanctity of marriage and the union of families. Costanza listened intently, her gaze fixed on Bosio's, finding reassurance in his steady presence.

When it came time for their vows, Bosio spoke first, his voice firm and deliberate. "I, Bosio, take you, Costanza, to be my wife. I promise to honor and protect you, to uphold the bonds of our families, and to stand beside you in all things."

Costanza's throat tightened, but she managed to speak her own vows with grace. "I, Costanza, take you, Bosio, to be my husband. I promise to be faithful and steadfast, to support you, and to honor the legacy of our union."

As the priest's final words echoed through the grand chamber, the guests erupted into polite applause. The sound was distant in Costanza's ears, her attention fixed solely on Bosio Sforza. He stepped closer, his dark eyes holding hers with a steady intensity that made her pulse quicken. Her heart raced—not from nerves, but from the weight of the moment.

Slowly, Bosio reached out and lifted the delicate lace veil that framed her face. The fabric fell back, revealing her features fully to him for the first time. Costanza held her breath, her hands clasped tightly in front of her, unsure of what he might see in her expression—anxiety, hope, or something she couldn't yet name.

His lips curved into the faintest smile, a flicker of warmth breaking through his composed demeanor. "You are radiant," he murmured, his voice low enough that only she could hear.

The compliment, simple as it was, sent a warmth coursing through her. Before she could respond, Bosio took another step forward, closing the space between them. Gently, as though mindful of the enormity of the act, he leaned down.

Costanza's breath hitched as his lips brushed hers—a soft, lingering touch that was both tender and resolute. For that brief moment, the weight of the day fell away. There were no whispered intrigues, no watchful eyes, only the quiet connection between them.

When he pulled back, his gaze lingered on her, searching her face for a reaction. Costanza found herself smiling, a small but genuine curve of her lips that she hoped conveyed both her gratitude and her resolve.

The applause swelled around them again as the priest declared, "You are now husband and wife."

Bosio extended his hand to her, and with newfound confidence, Costanza placed her hand in his. Together, they turned to face the crowd, their first steps as husband and wife marking the beginning of a union that would change both their lives forever.

The reception at the Farnese palace was a spectacle of Renaissance grandeur. Tables laden with roasted meats, fine wines, and delicate pastries stretched across the garden, beneath canopies of ivy and silk. Musicians played lively tunes as guests danced and mingled, their laughter mingling with the warm evening breeze.

Costanza sat at the head table beside Bosio, her earlier nerves replaced by a sense of cautious optimism. He leaned closer to her, his voice low enough that only she could hear.

"You handled today with remarkable grace," he said. "I hope it hasn't been too overwhelming."

"It has," she admitted with a small smile. "But I believe I'll survive."

His laughter was quiet but genuine, and for the first time, Costanza felt a flicker of ease in his presence.

As the evening wore on, a commotion at the palace's gates drew the attention of the guests. A messenger arrived, disheveled and out of breath, demanding to see Cardinal Alessandro Farnese. Alessandro excused himself from the festivities, his expression darkening as he read the parchment the man handed him.

The tension did not go unnoticed by Costanza, who exchanged a worried glance with Bosio. Moments later, Alessandro returned, his composure restored but his movements brisk.

"Is something amiss, Father?" Costanza asked quietly as he passed her table.

"Nothing that cannot wait," he replied, though his tone betrayed a hint of unease.

Bosio's gaze followed Alessandro as he disappeared into the villa. "It seems even a wedding cannot shield us from the realities of Rome," he said, his voice thoughtful.

Costanza nodded, her mind swirling with questions. Whatever had happened, it was clear their union was not just a personal milestone but a political one, entwined with the machinations of power that surrounded their families.

As the festivities began to wind down, Bosio and Costanza found themselves alone in the palace's garden. The stars above sparkled against the dark sky, their light reflected in the still waters of the fountain.

"I imagine this isn't how you pictured your wedding day," Bosio said, breaking the silence.

"No," Costanza admitted, her voice soft. "But perhaps it's fitting. Our lives were never going to be simple."

He studied her for a moment before replying. "You're right. But that doesn't mean they can't be meaningful."

Costanza turned to him, her gaze steady. "Then let's make them meaningful—together."

Bosio inclined his head, his expression thoughtful. "Agreed."

In that quiet moment, the weight of the day seemed to lift, leaving only the promise of what lay ahead. For better or worse, they were now partners in a world where loyalty and ambition were everything.

Chapter 23

The reception at the Farnese palace gradually quieted as the festivities wound down. The sound of music and laughter faded into the soft hum of nighttime. Servants moved discreetly, extinguishing lanterns and tidying the garden as the last guests departed. In her wedding night chambers, Costanza Farnese stood before the grand mirror, the lace of her wedding gown pooling around her feet as her maid gently unlaced the back of her bodice.

"You've had a long day, my lady," the maid said softly, her deft hands working to loosen the intricate ties. "Shall I stay with you a little while longer?"

Costanza shook her head, her voice steady but kind. "Thank you, Maria, but that won't be necessary."

As the maid curtsied and left the room, Costanza let out a breath she hadn't realized she was holding. She slipped into the silk chemise laid out for her, the fabric cool against her skin. The bedchamber, illuminated by the warm glow of several candles, felt both intimate and unfamiliar. Tonight, this room—this life—would no longer be hers alone.

The faint sound of footsteps on the stone floor announced his approach. Costanza turned toward the door just as it opened, revealing Bosio Sforza. He stepped inside, his movements deliberate, his dark gaze steady as it settled on her. He had removed the formal doublet he wore at the ceremony, his attire now simpler but no less refined.

For a moment, they stood apart, the soft glow of the candlelight casting shadows that danced across the room. Bosio's gaze met Costanza's, his dark eyes steady yet warm, as though he was silently offering her reassurance.

"You are breathtaking," he said quietly, his voice low and rich. "I feel as though the stars themselves could not outshine you tonight."

Costanza felt her breath catch, a warmth rising to her cheeks. "You flatter me, Signor Sforza," she replied softly, though her voice trembled slightly. "It has been a long day."

"Not flattery," he said, stepping closer, his movements deliberate but gentle. "Truth. I could say nothing at all, and the sight of you would still leave me humbled."

Her pulse quickened as he came to stand before her, his presence filling the space between them. "I've wondered all day what this moment would be like," she admitted, her words barely above a whisper.

"And now?" he asked, his voice soft, as though the world beyond this moment did not exist.

"And now," she replied, her gaze meeting his, "I feel as though the world has finally quieted."

As he approached, Costanza's nerves fluttered, but she found herself meeting his gaze without hesitation. He stopped a few paces from her, his expression thoughtful as though weighing his words.

"I know this union was not of your choosing," he said softly. "But it is one I intend to honor. I will not ask for more than you're ready to give."

Costanza blinked, his gentleness catching her off guard. In that moment, the formalities and expectations surrounding their marriage faded, leaving only the sincerity of his words.

The soft glow of the candles cast flickering shadows on the walls as Bosio reached for Costanza's hand, his touch warm and steady. For a moment, they stood in silence, the weight of the day fading as they looked at one another— not as two strangers bound by duty, but as two individuals at the beginning of something new.

He lifted her hand to his lips, pressing a soft kiss to her fingers before guiding her gently toward the bed. The layers of their formalities—

her silk chemise, his fine tunic—were shed with unhurried care, each movement a quiet promise. He paused, his dark eyes searching hers for any sign of hesitation.

When she gave a small, affirming nod, he leaned forward, his lips brushing hers with a tenderness that sent a shiver down her spine. Their kiss deepened slowly, a delicate exploration of trust and connection. His hand rested lightly at her waist, drawing her closer but never forcing, his touch speaking of both reverence and restraint.

Costanza's nerves eased as his warmth surrounded her, their breaths mingling as they lay together. The rhythm of their movements was gentle, guided by an unspoken understanding. Bosio's words, soft and steady, carried through the quiet: reassurances of her beauty, her strength, and the future they would build together.

His touch awakened sensations within her that she had never imagined, stirring emotions for which she had no words.

Her breath quickened, each stroke of his skilled hands sending waves of anticipation coursing through her.

When their connection reached its peak, it was with a quiet intensity that left them both breathless. She felt that moment was not about their bodies, as much as it was about the joining of their souls.

As they lay entwined, the room filled with the faint crackle of the dying fire, Costanza rested her head against Bosio's chest, the steady beat of his heart grounding her.

"This is only the beginning," he murmured, pressing a kiss to her temple.

Costanza closed her eyes, a small smile on her lips as she whispered, "I think I will love being your wife."

Chapter 24

The morning after the wedding dawned with the soft light of the Roman sun filtering through the ornate windows of the Farnese Palace. The air was thick with the scents of roses and lingering candle wax from the evening's festivities. Costanza Farnese, now Countessa Sforza, awoke to the sound of birds chirping outside her window and the muted hum of activity in the palace courtyard below.

She lay still for a moment, letting the reality of her new life settle around her. The previous day's events felt like a whirlwind—a grand ceremony, an opulent reception, and the intimate moments shared with Bosio Sforza. Now, in the quiet of the morning, the weight of her new role pressed gently upon her.

There was little time for lingering thoughts, however. Today, she and Bosio would journey to the Ruffini villa, her mother's estate on the outskirts of Rome. It was a place of cherished memories for Costanza, where she had spent many summers as a child. The villa would serve as a brief respite before they continued on to Santa Fiora, Bosio's ancestral home.

As servants moved efficiently through the corridors, packing trunks and preparing carriages, Costanza dressed in a simple yet elegant traveling gown of deep green velvet. The rich color complemented her dark hair, which was braided and coiled at the nape of her neck. She took a final look around her chambers—the gilded mirrors, the frescoed ceiling, the heavy silk drapes—all familiar yet now tinged with a sense of departure.

In the grand hall, Cardinal Alessandro Farnese awaited them. His posture was as commanding as ever, but there was a softness in his eyes as he approached his daughter.

"Your mother has gone ahead to the villa to make preparations," he said. "She insisted everything be perfect for your arrival."

Costanza smiled gently. "She has always cared for the smallest details."

Alessandro took her hands in his. "Remember, Costanza, as you step into this new life, the strength of our family goes with you. You carry not only the Farnese name but the hopes of our legacy."

"I will honor it, Father," she replied, meeting his gaze with steadfast resolve.

Bosio approached, inclining his head respectfully to Alessandro. "Cardinal, I assure you, Costanza's well-being is my utmost priority."

Alessandro nodded. "See that it remains so."

The carriage ride to the Ruffini villa was a short but pleasant journey through the Roman countryside. The landscape shifted from the bustling city streets to the gentle rolling hills dotted with cypress trees and vineyards.

Seated beside Bosio, Costanza felt a mix of emotions. The familiarity of the route brought back memories of carefree days spent exploring the villa's gardens and orchards. Yet, the presence of her husband beside her was a constant reminder of the new path she was forging.

Bosio glanced at her, his expression thoughtful. "You seem deep in thought. Are you anxious about returning to the villa?"

"Not anxious," she replied. "Reflective, perhaps. The Ruffini villa holds many memories for me."

He offered a reassuring smile. "Then it's fitting we visit there before heading to Santa Fiora. A way to bridge your past and our future."

She appreciated his understanding. "Yes, I believe so."

The sun cast a warm glow over the terracotta roofs of the Ruffini villa as they arrived. Lush gardens surrounded the estate, bursting with roses and jasmine that filled the air with their fragrant scent. Silvia Ruffini stood at the entrance, her face lighting up as the carriage approached.

"Welcome home, my dear," she said, embracing Costanza as she stepped down from the carriage.

"Thank you, Mother. It's good to be here, even if only for a short while."

Bosio greeted Silvia with a polite bow. "Signora Ruffini, thank you for hosting us."

"The pleasure is mine, Count Sforza," she replied graciously. "Please, make yourselves at home."

That evening, they dined in the villa's intimate dining room, its windows overlooking the gardens where twilight cast long shadows. The meal was a collection of Costanza's favorite dishes from childhood—roasted lamb with rosemary, fresh figs drizzled with honey, and delicate almond pastries.

As they ate, Silvia shared stories from Costanza's youth, anecdotes that brought laughter and a touch of embarrassment to her daughter.

"Mother, you'll have Bosio thinking I was a wild child," Costanza protested lightly after a particularly amusing tale of her climbing the orchard trees in search of the perfect apple.

Bosio chuckled. "On the contrary, it pleases me to learn more about your spirited nature."

Silvia reached across the table to squeeze Costanza's hand. "You have always had a strong will and a kind heart. Traits that will serve you well in your new life."

Later, Costanza and Bosio strolled through the moonlit gardens. The familiar paths were comforting to her, the rustling leaves and chirping crickets a soothing backdrop.

"This place holds a special charm," Bosio remarked, his gaze taking in the manicured hedges and blooming flowers.

"It does," Costanza agreed. "I used to imagine these gardens were a vast kingdom, and I was its queen."

He smiled at the image. "And now you will preside over Santa Fiora. Perhaps not a kingdom, but a place where your influence can make a real difference."

She glanced at him, appreciating the sentiment. "I hope so. Tell me more about Santa Fiora. What should I expect?"

Bosio considered her question. "It's a land of rugged beauty—rolling hills, dense forests, and clear streams. The people are hardworking and loyal. The villa is not as grand as the palaces of Rome, but it has a history and warmth that I cherish."

"I look forward to seeing it," she said genuinely.

As they prepared to retire for the night, Costanza felt a sense of peace. The visit to the

Ruffini villa had bridged the gap between her past and the uncertain future. Surrounded by the comforts of her childhood home and the steady presence of Bosio, she felt more prepared for the journey ahead.

"Rest well," Bosio said softly. "Tomorrow, we continue to Santa Fiora."

"Goodnight," she replied, offering a small smile. "And thank you for indulging this visit. It means a great deal to me."

He inclined his head. "It was my pleasure."

Chapter 25

The journey from Rome to Santa Fiora began before dawn, the first light of the day casting the countryside in hues of soft gold and gray. Costanza sat beside Bosio Sforza in the lead carriage, her gaze fixed on the road ahead. The villa of her childhood and the bustling vibrancy of Rome had faded into memory, replaced by the unknown expanse of Tuscany awaiting her.

Though she had traveled short distances outside the city, this was the first time she ventured so far into the countryside. The rugged beauty of the landscape was unlike anything she had seen before. Rolling hills stretched endlessly in every direction, their slopes dotted with olive groves and vineyards. The occasional stone villa stood solitary among the fields, its terracotta roof glowing warmly in the morning light.

"It's beautiful," Costanza murmured, her voice tinged with awe.

Bosio, seated beside her, glanced at her with a faint smile. "Tuscany has a way of humbling even the grandest city dwellers. I'm glad you see its charm."

"It feels wild," she said thoughtfully, her eyes following the path of a hawk circling above. "Untamed, compared to Rome's order."

"Santa Fiora has its own kind of order," he said. "But yes, life here is closer to the earth."

As the hours wore on, the road grew rougher, winding through dense forests and over narrow bridges spanning swift streams. The air, sweet with the scent of wildflowers in the valleys, turned cooler as they climbed into the hills.

Midway through the journey, dark clouds began gathering on the horizon. By the time they reached a small village for a brief rest, the first drops of rain had begun to fall. Bosio directed the servants to cover the luggage and secure the carriages, but the storm arrived quickly, its heavy downpour turning the dirt roads into slippery tracks of mud.

The carriages pressed on, their progress slowed by the worsening conditions. Inside, Costanza gripped the edge of the seat as the wheels jolted over uneven terrain. The once-serene countryside now felt hostile, the rain pounding against the windows and the wind howling through the trees.

As they rounded a sharp bend in the road, the lead carriage skidded, the wheels slipping precariously close to the edge of a steep embankment. The driver shouted, yanking the reins to steady the horses, but the carriage lurched violently. Costanza cried out as she was thrown against the side, Bosio's arm moving swiftly to steady her.

"Hold on!" he commanded, his voice firm and reassuring.

The carriage came to an abrupt halt, the horses rearing and whinnying in protest. Outside, the servants rushed to secure the vehicle, their voices muffled by the storm. Bosio opened the door and stepped out into the rain, issuing orders with calm authority.

Costanza remained inside, her heart pounding. The near-disaster left her shaken, and for the first time since leaving Rome, she felt the sharp sting of homesickness. She pressed a hand to her chest, willing herself to breathe deeply and calm her racing thoughts.

Bosio returned moments later, his dark hair plastered to his forehead from the rain. He knelt before her, his hand resting gently on her knee.

"Are you hurt?" he asked, his voice softer now.

"No," she managed, though her voice trembled. "But… I was frightened."

"As was I," he admitted, his expression earnest. "But we're safe now. The road ahead will be difficult, but I promise we will reach Santa Fiora."

His honesty and steady presence comforted her, though the ache for the familiarity of home lingered. "Thank you," she said quietly, meeting his gaze. "For keeping me safe."

Hours later, the storm began to wane, and the rugged landscape of Santa Fiora came into view. The villa stood atop a hill, its stone walls weathered but strong, framed by dense forests and the soft green of pastureland. A winding path led to the gates, where servants awaited their arrival with lanterns in hand.

As the carriage came to a stop, Costanza stepped out onto the gravel drive, her gown damp and her spirits heavy. The villa was smaller and simpler than the Ruffini villa, but there was a quiet beauty in its sturdy lines and the way it seemed to grow naturally from the land around it.

Bosio stood beside her, his hand resting lightly on her back. "This is your home now," he said, his voice both reassuring and resolute.

Costanza looked up at the villa, her emotions a mix of exhaustion, apprehension, and determination. "It is different," she said finally.

"It is," Bosio replied. "But it is ours."

As the servants ushered them inside, the warmth of the villa's hearths and the scent of fresh bread began to ease Costanza's lingering unease. She would need time to adjust and learn the rhythms of this new life and the people who inhabited it. But for now, she allowed herself to rest, the fire's glow softening the edges of the day's trials.

That night, as she lay in bed listening to the rain pattering against the windows, she whispered a silent prayer for strength. The journey to Santa Fiora had been more challenging than she anticipated, and the ache for the familiar remained. Yet there was something in Bosio's steadiness, in the resilience of the land itself, that gave her hope.

Tomorrow would be a new day, and she resolved to face it with the fortitude her family had always instilled in her. Whatever Santa Fiora held, she would meet it with grace and courage.

Chapter 26

The transition to Santa Fiora had not been without its challenges. For Costanza Farnese, the adjustment from her upbringing in the opulence of Rome to the more practical, earthbound life as Countessa Sforza required a balancing act. She had always been quick-witted and observant, qualities that now served her well. Yet, the weight of her new role—both as a wife and as the lady of the estate—was unlike anything she had ever experienced.

The sound of church bells rang out over the hills of Santa Fiora, signaling the beginning of her first full day as Countessa. The air smelled of damp earth and wood smoke, a far cry from the perfumed gardens of her family's villa in Rome. Standing at the window of her chambers, Costanza gazed out at the sprawling countryside that stretched to the horizon.

"Is it what you imagined?" Bosio asked, entering the room quietly.

She turned to him, her expression thoughtful. "It is… simpler," she said, "But no less beautiful."

He smiled faintly, his presence a steadying force in her new life. "It is yours now, as much as it is mine. If you need anything—guidance, assistance—do not hesitate to ask."

Costanza appreciated his kindness, but she had no intention of relying on him more than necessary. She had been raised to command respect, to carry the weight of her family name. Now, she intended to do the same for the Sforza family.

Her first task as Countessa was to meet the staff who managed the estate. A formal gathering was held in the main hall, where the servants stood in orderly rows, their faces a mix of curiosity and deference.

"This is your new Countessa," Bosio announced, his tone both warm and authoritative. "She will lead this household alongside me, and you will afford her the same respect you show me."

Costanza stepped forward, her posture straight, her voice calm but clear. "I am honored to be here among you," she said. "I know the Sforza name carries a legacy of strength and honor. Together, we will ensure that legacy endures."

As she spoke, her eyes moved over the faces before her, noting the subtle differences in their reactions. Some looked reassured, while others remained cautious, as though reserving judgment. Costanza knew that winning their loyalty would take time and effort, and she welcomed the challenge.

The Sforza family itself presented its own set of complexities. Bosio's elder sister, Elena, resided at the villa and managed the estate in his absence before Costanza's arrival. A woman of sharp intellect and strong opinions, Elena regarded Costanza with polite skepticism.

At their first private meeting over tea, Elena wasted no time in probing her new sister-in-law. "You've come from Rome, from a family of great wealth and influence. How will you adapt to life here, in a place where practicality often outweighs prestige?"

Costanza met her gaze evenly. "By learning from those who know it best," she replied. "And by bringing my own strengths to complement what is already established."

Elena tilted her head, a hint of amusement playing on her lips. "A diplomatic answer. You'll need more than diplomacy here, Countessa."

"Good," Costanza said with a small smile. "Because I have more than diplomacy to offer."

Though the exchange was tense, Costanza sensed that Elena respected her resolve. It was not friendship—not yet—but it was a beginning.

In the weeks that followed, Costanza threw herself into the responsibilities of running the estate. She spent mornings meeting with the steward, Giovanni, to review the estate's finances and ensure the proper management of the land and its tenants. She visited the vineyards and olive groves, speaking with the workers and learning the rhythms of their labor. Though her gowns were always immaculate and her poise unshaken, she did not shy away from the realities of the land.

"Your attention to detail surprises me," Giovanni remarked one afternoon as they walked through the orchard. "Many in your position would leave such matters to the steward."

"Perhaps," Costanza replied, brushing her gloved hand against the bark of an olive tree. "But this estate is not just my husband's; it is mine. How can I lead if I do not understand what I am leading?"

Her answer seemed to satisfy him, and over time, Lorenzo became one of her staunchest allies.

In the evenings, Costanza and Bosio dined together in the villa's grand yet understated dining room. Their conversations ranged from the affairs of the estate to the broader political landscape of Tuscany. Though their marriage had begun as a union of necessity, a quiet respect began to blossom between them.

"You're adapting well," Bosio said one evening, his tone carrying a note of admiration. "More quickly than I expected."

"I had little choice," Costanza replied, though her smile softened the words. "But I admit, there is a certain satisfaction in it."

"And Elena?" he asked, raising an eyebrow. "How does she find you?"

"She tests me," Costanza said simply. "But I think she is beginning to approve. Or at least, she has stopped looking at me as though I might ruin everything."

Bosio laughed, a rare and genuine sound. "If you've won over Elena, then you've already done the impossible."

By the end of her first year as Countessa of Santa Fiora, Costanza had established herself as a capable and compassionate leader. Her strength of character, inherited from her Farnese lineage, combined with her willingness to learn, earned her the respect of the household and the tenants.

Yet, even as she settled into her new life, she often found herself thinking of Rome—of her father's ambitious plans and her brothers' growing roles in the Farnese legacy. She was far from home, but she was no less a Farnese. And as the seasons turned, she began to see Santa Fiora not as a place of exile, but as the stage for her own ambitions.

Chapter 27

The soft knock at the door of her sitting room came just as Costanza was finishing her correspondence with one of the local merchants. She looked up to see a steward, Giovanni, entering with a folded parchment sealed with the familiar crest of the Ruffini family. Her heart lifted slightly at the sight.

"A letter from Rome, my lady," Giovanni said, bowing as he handed it to her.

"Thank you," she replied, setting aside her pen and breaking the seal with careful fingers. She unfolded the parchment, her mother's elegant handwriting bringing a flood of warmth and a touch of unease.

Dearest Costanza,
I hope this letter finds you well and settling into your new life in Santa Fiora. Not a day

passes that I do not think of you and pray for your happiness. I miss your presence here in Rome, as do your brothers, though they are both so busy with their own pursuits that they would never admit it outright.

Pier Luigi is proving to be as headstrong as ever. Your father has arranged for him to begin formal lessons in diplomacy under one of his trusted advisors. It is no easy task, as Pier Luigi's ambitions often lead him to push boundaries, but Alessandro remains hopeful that with proper guidance, he will channel his energy wisely.

Ranuccio, on the other hand, grows quieter by the day, immersed in his studies of theology. He reminds me more of your father with each passing month—calm, contemplative, and deliberate. Your father believes he may one day enter the Church, a prospect that brings him great pride.

As for your father, his work in the Vatican keeps him constantly occupied. The politics of the Holy See are as turbulent as ever, and tensions among the cardinals grow with each passing day. Pope Leo X's indulgences have drawn criticism, and whispers of dissent can be heard even within Rome. There is talk of reform, but it is unclear whether the Church has the will to act decisively.

Closer to home, your father worries about the growing unrest among the people. Taxes have been raised again to fund the Pope's grand projects, and many of the poorer families are struggling to survive. Though your father does not speak of it often, I know he carries the burden of these tensions heavily.

On a brighter note, I have taken it upon myself to begin improvements to the Ruffini villa. The gardens are being expanded, and I have commissioned a new fountain for the courtyard—a small indulgence, but one that I hope will bring some joy to our home.

I hope that you will write soon and tell me of your life in Santa Fiora. Is the countryside as beautiful as I imagine? How are you finding your place among the Sforzas? I long to hear your thoughts, my dear daughter. Remember, though distance separates us, my love for you remains as strong as ever.

With all my heart,
Your mother,
Silvia Ruffini

As Costanza folded the letter, a mix of emotions welled within her. The mention of her brothers brought a small smile to her lips—she could picture Pier Luigi's fiery determination and Ranuccio's quiet intellect so clearly, even from afar. Yet the news of Rome's unrest weighed heavily on her. She had grown up in a world of wealth and privilege, but her mother's words reminded her of the struggles faced by so many within the city.

Her father's involvement in Vatican politics was no surprise, but the talk of criticism and reform left her uneasy. The Church's stability—or lack thereof—was not just a religious matter; it had the power to shape alliances, wealth, and even the fate of families like her own.

She rose from her seat and moved to the window, gazing out at the rolling hills of Santa Fiora. The countryside was indeed beautiful, but it felt so far removed from the intricate web of power and tension that was Rome. She wondered how her father was truly faring amidst the turmoil and whether her brothers understood the weight of the paths being laid before them.

As the sun dipped lower in the sky, Costanza turned back to her desk, retrieving a fresh sheet of parchment. She dipped her quill in ink and began her reply.

Dearest Mother,
Your letter was a balm to my heart, a reminder of the home and family I hold so dear...

She paused, thinking carefully about her words. Though she could not be in Rome, she could still offer her support through her writing, a thread that would keep her tied to the life she had left behind.

Chapter 28

The flickering candlelight cast long shadows on the ornate walls of the Farnese palace as Costanza sat in her father's study, her curiosity piqued by a snippet of conversation she had overheard earlier in the day. Her husband, Bosio, and her father had spoken of alliances and legacies, their tones hushed but animated. Amid their words, one name stood out: Giulia "la Bella" Farnese.

"Father," Costanza said tentatively, breaking the silence. Her father looked up from his letters, his expression softening at the sight of her. "Why is Aunt Giulia still spoken of with such reverence—and scandal?"

Alessandro Farnese leaned back in his chair, a faint smile tugging at his lips. "Ah, Giulia," he said, his voice carrying a blend of affection and amusement. "She was as much a mystery in life as she is in memory. You could say she laid the foundation for much of what we are today."

Intrigued, Costanza pressed further. "What do you mean? What did she do?"

Alessandro gestured for her to sit, folding his hands as he began his story. "Giulia, my dear sister, was renowned for her beauty—a gift that earned her the nickname 'la Bella.' But she was more than just a pretty face. She became the mistress of Rodrigo Borgia, who later ascended as Pope Alexander VI. Through her, the Farnese family entered the orbit of papal power. It was her presence in his court that cemented the Farnese name among the great families of Rome."

Costanza's brow furrowed. "But to be a mistress…wasn't that a scandal? Did it not harm the family?"

Her father chuckled lightly, though there was a trace of bitterness in his tone. "In those days, power often came wrapped in scandal. Giulia understood the game better than most. She used her beauty and wit to secure patronage for our family. Through her influence, she elevated us from the shadows into the light of the Vatican. Without her, my path might never have been possible."

Costanza nodded slowly, absorbing his words. Later that evening, she sought out her mother, Silvia, hoping for a different perspective. She found her in the solarium, working on an embroidery of the Farnese crest.

"Mother, what do you remember of Aunt Giulia?" Costanza asked, sitting beside her.

Silvia glanced at her daughter, her fingers pausing over the needle. "Giulia was a woman ahead of her time," Silvia said softly. "She knew how to navigate a world that often dismissed women as mere ornaments. Yes, she was a mistress, but she was also a strategist, a diplomat in her own right. She ensured that her family's name was always spoken in the corridors of power."

"She must have been strong," Costanza mused.

"She was," Silvia affirmed. "But strength comes at a cost. The Church and society—judged her harshly. Yet, she bore it all with grace, knowing that her sacrifices paved the way for her brothers, her descendants…for you."

The following morning, Costanza wandered through the villa, her thoughts consumed by her aunt's story. She found herself in a lesser-used gallery where portraits of the Farnese ancestors lined the walls. One painting in particular caught her eye—a young woman with flowing auburn hair, her gaze piercing and enigmatic. Giulia.

Costanza stood before the portrait, studying the face that had shaped her family's destiny. She could see the allure in her features, the intelligence in her eyes. It was not difficult to imagine how such a woman had captivated one of the most powerful men in the Church.

As she traced the delicate frame of the painting with her fingers, a thought struck her. Giulia's story was not so different from her own. Both women had navigated a world dominated by men, using their strengths to secure a place for their families. Where Giulia had wielded beauty and influence, Costanza wielded patience and resolve.

"She endured," Costanza whispered to herself. "And so will I."

When she returned to the hall, the weight of her family's legacy was heavy, but it was a burden she had been born to carry. Like Giulia, she would ensure the Farnese name thrived—not through scandal, but through the quiet strength of a woman who understood the cost of greatness.

In the weeks that followed, Costanza found herself returning to Giulia's portrait, drawing inspiration from the woman who had turned scandal into triumph. For the Farnese, shadows were not something to be feared. They were a source of power, a place where light could be born.

And Costanza vowed that she, too, would leave her mark in the annals of their legacy—one that echoed not just Giulia's courage, but the strength of every Farnese who had come before.

Chapter 29

The crisp autumn air of Santa Fiora in 1518 carried a sense of anticipation through the villa. Servants bustled quietly, their movements purposeful yet hushed as though the very walls understood the gravity of the moment. Inside the bedchamber, Costanza Farnese, now Countessa Sforza, lay surrounded by midwives and her trusted attendants. Her labor had begun at dawn, and though the hours stretched into the afternoon, her resolve remained steadfast.

"Breathe, my lady," the midwife urged, her tone steady yet soothing. "You're doing well."

Costanza gripped the edge of the bed, her face damp with effort but her eyes focused. She had always been determined, and today was no exception. She was bringing forth the heir to the Sforza line, the child who would symbolize the union of two powerful families.

In the adjoining sitting room, Silvia Ruffini, Costanza's mother, paced anxiously. She had arrived in Santa Fiora weeks earlier, determined to be at her daughter's side for this pivotal moment. Though accustomed to the challenges of motherhood herself, watching her eldest endure the trials of childbirth filled her with a mixture of pride and worry.

The door creaked open, and Bosio Sforza entered, his expression calm but his shoulders tense. "How is she?" he asked.

"She's strong," Silvia replied, though her voice wavered slightly. "Stronger than I was during my first. She will be fine."

Bosio nodded, though his worry was evident. "I've never felt so powerless," he admitted quietly. "She carries the future of our family in her hands."

"And she will deliver it," Silvia said firmly. "She is Farnese, after all."

As the afternoon sun dipped toward the horizon, a sharp cry echoed through the villa. The tension in the air broke, replaced by murmurs of relief and joy. Moments later, the midwife emerged, her face glowing with satisfaction.

"A boy," she announced. "Healthy and strong."

Bosio and Silvia exchanged a glance before rushing into the room. Costanza lay back against the pillows, her face pale but radiant. In her arms was a swaddled infant, his tiny fists curling and uncurling as he let out a soft whimper.

"Meet your son," Costanza said, her voice hoarse but filled with pride.

Bosio knelt beside her, his large hands trembling slightly as he touched the baby's head. "Guido Ascanio," he murmured, his voice filled with reverence. "You have done so well, Costanza."

Silvia approached, her heart swelling as she looked at her grandson. "He has your strength," she said softly, brushing her fingers over the baby's cheek. "And the Sforza fire, I imagine."

Costanza managed a weak smile. "He will have both," she said. "Strength and fire. It is his birthright."

As the news spread, the villa erupted in quiet celebration. Servants toasted with wine, and the chapel bells rang out to mark the birth of the heir to the Sforza estate. Inside, Costanza rested while Silvia and Bosio remained by her side, marveling at the tiny life cradled in her arms.

"Rome will be pleased," Silvia said after a while. "An heir strengthens your position, and your father will be proud."

Costanza looked at her mother, her expression thoughtful. "Do you think he'll come to meet his grandson?"

Silvia hesitated, then shook her head gently. "Your father's duties in the Vatican are many.

But know that his pride in you is as constant as the sunrise."

Costanza nodded, her thoughts briefly turning to her family in Rome—her father's unyielding ambition, Pier Luigi's fiery determination, Ranuccio's quiet devotion. They were far away, yet she felt their presence in this moment, their legacy now carried forward by her son.

As the household settled for the night, Costanza remained awake, gazing at Guido Ascanio as he slept in a cradle beside her bed. Bosio sat nearby, his eyes heavy with exhaustion, but his presence grounded her.

"Do you think he'll love this place as much as you do?" Costanza asked softly, her gaze still on the baby.

"He will," Bosio replied. "Because it is his. Just as it is ours."

Costanza reached for his hand, their fingers intertwining. In this moment, despite the trials of childbirth and the weight of expectations, she felt a quiet contentment. Her life had changed irrevocably, but in her son's tiny form, she saw the future—a future she was determined to shape with strength and grace.

Chapter 30

Rome 1519

The grand Basilica of San Pietro in Montorio was adorned with flowers and silk banners in the colors of the Farnese and Orsini families. The scent of incense filled the air as Rome's elite gathered to witness the union. Costanza sat near the front, her gown of soft gold brocade shimmering in the candlelight. Beside her, Bosio offered a reassuring presence, his hand resting lightly on hers.

Pier Luigi stood at the altar, a vision of confidence in his crimson and gold doublet. His bride, Gerolama Orsini, moved gracefully down the aisle in a gown of pale blue, her veil trailing like a river of starlight. The ceremony unfolded with all the grandeur befitting two of Italy's most powerful families, every word and gesture steeped in meaning.

Costanza's heart swelled with pride as the vows were exchanged. Her brother, once impulsive and brash, now carried himself with a quiet dignity that spoke of his growing maturity. Yet she couldn't help but wonder if he felt as conflicted as she had on her wedding day—caught between duty and hope, between family and the self.

The Farnese palace overflowed with life as the celebration continued late into the evening. Long tables groaned under the weight of roasted meats, sugared fruits, and fine wines. Musicians played in the corner, their melodies weaving through the hum of conversation and laughter.

Costanza moved through the crowd with practiced ease, her polite smiles and careful words masking her exhaustion. She spotted Pier Luigi near a balcony, his wine goblet raised in a toast with one of Gerolama's relatives. As their eyes met, he excused himself and strode over.

"Sister," he said, pulling her into a quick embrace. "You came."

"Of course," she replied. "Did you think I would let you begin married life without my approval?"

He chuckled. "I suppose not. And Bosio—has he forgiven me for stealing you back to Rome?"

Costanza glanced at her husband, who was deep in conversation across the room. "I think he understands. Though he's learned to share me with the Farnese ambitions."

Pier Luigi smirked. "And how is married life treating you?"

"Well enough," she said. "Though I suspect Gerolama will keep you busier than Santa Fiora keeps me."

"Likely," Pier Luigi admitted, his expression softening. "But she's a good match. Our families need this."

Costanza placed a hand on his arm, her voice quieter now. "And what about you, Pier Luigi? Are you happy?"

He hesitated, the mask of confidence slipping for a moment. "I don't know if happiness matters as much as doing what's right for the family."

Costanza sighed, understanding all too well. "Then I hope you find both. You deserve it."

As the evening wore on, Costanza stepped outside onto the terrace, seeking a moment of quiet. The cool night air wrapped around her, carrying the faint sounds of the city below. Rome stretched out before her, its lights flickering like stars scattered across the earth.

Bosio joined her, his presence steady and grounding. "It was a beautiful ceremony," he said, offering her a goblet of wine.

"It was," she agreed, her voice thoughtful. "Pier Luigi has grown, hasn't he? He seems ready for this."

"He does," Bosio said. "And so do you."

Costanza turned to him, her expression curious. "Do you think so? Sometimes, I wonder if I'm still learning what it means to be a Sforza."

Bosio smiled faintly. "Being a Sforza doesn't mean forgetting you're a Farnese. You carry both, Costanza, and you do it well."

His words brought a sense of peace, and as she gazed back at the city, Costanza allowed herself to simply exist in the moment. The journey back to Santa Fiora would be long, but for now, she was home—among her family, her past, and the legacy she carried forward.

Chapter 31

1520

The summer air in Santa Fiora carried the scent of blooming wildflowers, but within the villa, the atmosphere was filled with hushed excitement. A messenger had arrived from Rome, bearing news that Gerolama Orsini, Pier Luigi's wife, had given birth to a son. The boy had been named Alessandro, after his grandfather.

Costanza sat in the shaded garden, the letter clasped in her hand. The words, written in Pier Luigi's confident script, radiated pride and joy.

"Costanza, my son is strong and healthy. We have named him Alessandro, in honor of Father. This boy is the future of our family, and I cannot wait for you to meet him."

She smiled, imagining her brother holding his newborn son. Her children played nearby, their laughter echoing through the villa's tranquil grounds. Three little ones, each a bundle of curiosity and energy, filled her life with joy. Two-year-old Guido eagerly swung a small wooden stick, mimicking the moves of a swordsman with all the determination his young age could muster. Nearby, one-year-old Francesca and baby Giulia sat amidst a patch of daisies, their tiny hands exploring the delicate petals. Francesca's delighted giggles joined Giulia's soft coos, blending with the gentle rustle of the leaves in the breeze.

The sound of approaching footsteps drew her from her thoughts. Bosio appeared, his steady presence as grounding as ever. He carried a goblet of wine, setting it gently on the table beside her before sitting down.

"Good news from Rome?" he asked, his voice warm.

"Pier Luigi has a son," Costanza replied, her smile widening. "They've named him Alessandro."

Bosio nodded, his hand covering hers. "Your brother must be overjoyed. And you?"

"I am so happy for him," she said softly, turning to watch their children. "It's a blessing for the family."

Bosio followed her gaze, his expression thoughtful. "Our family is growing strong,

Costanza. Not just in Rome, but here as well. You've given us so much already."

She turned her hand to intertwine her fingers with his, feeling the quiet reassurance in his touch. "I only wish I could share the joy every day with my brother. He would have loved to see all of them growing so quickly."

"He would," Bosio agreed, his voice steady. "And they carry his legacy as much as ours. Alessandro, Pier Luigi, all of them—they're part of something far bigger than just us."

Costanza nodded, her smile turning wistful. "It's overwhelming sometimes, isn't it? To think of the weight our name carries."

Bosio leaned closer, pressing a kiss to her temple. "You bear it with grace, Costanza. And you've created something beautiful here, in Santa Fiora—a haven for all of us."

Later that evening, Costanza penned a letter to Pier Luigi, her words filled with love and congratulations. She included stories of her own children—how little Francesca had taken her first steps, and how Guido had already begun to mimic his father's courage. She sealed the letter with the Sforza crest, whispering a prayer for her brother's new son and for the future their family would share.

As the sun dipped below the horizon, Costanza watched her children play with their father from the terrace, her heart full. The Farnese name was flourishing, its legacy extending across Rome and beyond. But here in Santa Fiora, amid the golden light and the laughter of her children, she found her truest joy.

As time went by, news reached Santa Fiora of Emperor Charles V's next decisive move—the convening of the Diet of Worms in January 1521. The name Martin Luther had spread like wildfire, and his criticisms of the Church sowed discord across Europe.

Costanza received the news during her daily routine, handed another letter by a messenger. This time, the seal bore the crest of a trusted family ally in Rome.

"Luther's teachings have been condemned," she read aloud to Bosio later that evening as they sat by the fire. "The Edict of Worms declares him an outlaw and his writings heretical. The emperor is trying to unify his territories under the Church's authority."

Bosio leaned forward, his gaze steady. "But the damage has already been done. Luther's ideas have taken root. Even the emperor cannot control the spread of such a movement."

Costanza frowned, her thoughts lingering on her father and brothers in Rome. "This will make things more dangerous for the Church. Reformist ideas don't vanish because they are condemned. They thrive in secret."

"You're right," Bosio agreed. "And the Church will have to adapt—or risk losing its grip entirely."

~

By April, another letter arrived from Rome. Costanza was in the midst of managing estate affairs when Bosio interrupted her with news of the emperor's latest decision.

"Charles has appointed his brother, Ferdinand, as Archduke of Austria," he said. "It's a clear move to strengthen the Habsburg presence in Central Europe."

"And to secure his own position as emperor," Costanza added thoughtfully. "By delegating power to Ferdinand, he consolidates his empire while ensuring loyalty from within his own family."

Bosio nodded. "It's a bold move, but one that could backfire if Ferdinand decides to assert too much independence. The Habsburgs are known for their unity, but even they are not immune to division."

Costanza sighed, her mind drifting back to her father. "And Rome must once again navigate these waters, caught between supporting the emperor and maintaining its own authority."

Bosio placed a hand on hers. "Your father has seen many storms. He will guide the Farnese through this one as well."

That evening, Costanza wrote her father a reply. She shared her thoughts on the political landscape, her words measured yet insightful. Though far from Rome, she felt deeply connected to the forces shaping Europe and the Church. Her child would be born into a world defined by these changes, and she resolved to stay informed and engaged.

As she sealed the letter, she gazed out the window at the moonlit hills of Santa Fiora. The world was shifting, its old certainties giving way to new realities. Yet within her, she carried a life—a promise of the future—and that gave her hope amidst the turmoil.

Chapter 32

1521

The summer heat of Santa Fiora pressed heavy on the villa, the air still except for the occasional rustle of leaves stirred by a faint breeze. Costanza Farnese, a few months away from the birth of her fourth child, paced the sunlit courtyard, her thoughts filled with anticipation. A messenger had arrived earlier that morning bearing news from Rome, where her brother Pier Luigi Farnese awaited the birth of his second child.

Costanza had always known that the Farnese legacy was bound to expand, but the thought of becoming an aunt again brought a curious sense of excitement. It was a reminder that their family, despite its tangled web of alliances and politics, continued to thrive.

As the afternoon sun reached its zenith, a servant approached Costanza in the courtyard, holding a scroll sealed with the crest of the Farnese family. Her heart quickened as she broke the seal and unfolded the parchment, the familiar script of her father, Cardinal Alessandro Farnese, immediately catching her eye.

Dearest Costanza,

Today, your brother Pier Luigi welcomes a daughter into the world. Vittoria Farnese, named for our family's noble forebears, is strong and healthy, and both she and her mother, Gerolama, are resting well. This moment fills me with pride, for it secures another generation of the Farnese legacy—a legacy I know will endure through the strength of our bloodline.

Pier Luigi has already begun to dream of Vittoria's future. With our guidance, I have no doubt she will rise to prominence in the courts, as all Farnese are destined to do.

You, my dear, will soon bring another child into this family. These children will carry forward all that we have worked for, and I trust they will one day stand united as heirs to our name.

With all my love,
Your father,
Alessandro Farnese

Costanza read the letter twice, her heart swelling with pride and joy. The Farnese family had faced its share of struggles, but this moment felt like a triumph—a beacon of hope in a world fraught with ambition and conflict.

That evening, Costanza retired to her writing desk, the parchment illuminated by the soft glow of candlelight. She dipped her quill into the ink and began a letter to Pier Luigi, her mind brimming with thoughts of the family they were building together.

Dearest Pier Luigi,

I write to you with great joy in my heart upon hearing of Vittoria's birth. Though I am far from Rome, I feel the bond of our family stronger than ever. I know you are an exceptional father, and I trust that Vittoria will grow under your guidance into a young woman worthy of our name.

As I prepare for another arrival of my own, I find comfort in knowing that our children will grow alongside one another, carrying forward the dreams of the Farnese and Sforza families alike. I pray that they will be as close as siblings, united in strength and loyalty.

May this new chapter bring you peace and happiness, dear brother. Give my regards to Gerolama and kiss young Alessandro and Vittoria for me.

With all my love,
Costanza

As she sealed the letter, Costanza placed a hand on her own swelling belly. The unborn child within her seemed to stir as if in response to her thoughts. In a few months, she too would hold a newborn child in her arms—a child who would share the world with Vittoria Farnese, a child who would carry forward the intertwined legacies of the Farnese and Sforza names.

The villa was quiet that night, the stars above glittering in a vast sky. Costanza stepped onto the balcony and looked out at the rolling hills of Santa Fiora, her mind filled with visions of the future. In the distance, the faint hum of cicadas filled the air, a comforting reminder of life's persistent rhythm.

Though she was far from Rome, Costanza felt the threads of her family's destiny pulling her closer. With every birth, every union, the Farnese legacy grew stronger. And in that thought, she found solace—an enduring pride in the family she had come from and the one she was building.

Chapter 33

The early winter air settled over the hills of Santa Fiora, a crisp stillness accompanying the season, but within the villa, the atmosphere was heavy with anticipation. Costanza Farnese, seated at her writing desk, glanced toward the cradle near the window where her new born son, Alessandro, slept peacefully. Her hand lingered on a ribbon tied around a folded parchment—her father's letter, delivered earlier that day.

Though the joys of motherhood filled her days, her thoughts now drifted to the words of Cardinal Alessandro Farnese, news that reached beyond the quiet confines of her new life in Santa Fiora to the heart of Rome itself. Taking a deep breath, she untied the ribbon and carefully unfolded the parchment, her eyes scanning the elegant script that carried tidings of family and faith, of politics and power.

Dearest Costanza,

Much has happened in recent weeks that I feel you must know. The Holy Father, Pope Leo X, has passed from this life. His death has cast a shadow over the Vatican, but it has also opened the path for a new shepherd of the Church.

After much deliberation, the cardinals have elected Adrian of Utrecht as our new pope. He has taken the name Adrian VI, and with his ascension comes a wave of reformist intentions. Adrian is unlike his predecessors. He is austere, a scholar, and deeply committed to addressing the corruption that has plagued the Church. Yet his foreign origins and lack of familiarity with Roman politics have already made him a target of resistance.

Here in Rome, the atmosphere is tense. Many within the Curia bristle at Adrian's attempts to reform their ways, while others, like myself, see an opportunity to restore the Church's moral authority. Yet I cannot ignore the whispers of dissent, the subtle sabotage of his efforts. Even as he takes the throne of Saint Peter, the city remains a crucible of ambition and power.

Your brothers are well. Pier Luigi continues his training, his fiery nature as unyielding as ever. Ranuccio, by contrast, grows ever more contemplative, his studies in theology drawing the attention of my peers. Both send their regards, though I suspect Pier Luigi's are grudging at best.

*My thoughts are often with you, my dear
daughter, as you prepare to bring new life into
this world. Know that your family stands with
you, even from afar.*
   With all my love,
   Your father,
   Alessandro Farnese

Costanza placed the letter down and let out a
long breath. News of Pope Leo X's death and the
election of Adrian VI brought a whirlwind of
emotions. The Farnese family had always
navigated the delicate balance of Church politics
with skill, but the ascension of a reformist pope
was sure to shake the foundations of power in
Rome.

Her thoughts were interrupted by Bosio
entering the room. He paused when he saw her
pensive expression.

"A letter from Rome?" he asked, stepping
closer.

"Yes," she replied, handing it to him. "From
my father. It seems the Vatican is entering a
period of change."

Bosio read the letter quickly, his brow
furrowing. "Adrian VI," he murmured. "A
foreign pope in a city that prides itself on its
own."

"And a reformer at that," Costanza added. "It
will unsettle many, including those who have
benefited from the Church's... excesses."

Bosio nodded thoughtfully. "And your father? Where does he stand in this?"

"He supports the reforms, at least in principle," Costanza said. "But I sense he is cautious. Rome does not change easily, and those who push too hard risk being undone."

Bosio sat beside her, his hand brushing hers gently. "Your family has always been adept at surviving Rome's storms. Still, this news will ripple far beyond the city."

Costanza tilted her head, studying his face. "And here? What does it mean for Santa Fiora?"

"For now, little," Bosio admitted. "But if Adrian's reforms begin to weaken the Church's authority or alienate its supporters, it could disrupt the balance of power across Italy. Families like ours depend on alliances with Rome to maintain our influence. A fractured Church benefits no one."

As the evening descended upon the villa, Costanza found herself walking through the gardens, her thoughts heavy. The political intrigue of Rome was far from the peaceful hills of Santa Fiora, yet it felt ever-present in her life. She thought of her father, maneuvering carefully through the Vatican's corridors, and of her brothers, each carving their own path in a world fraught with expectations.

Her hand rested gently on the ribbon of her shawl as her thoughts turned to her children. What kind of world would they inherit? Would it be one of opportunity, shaped by the Farnese and

Sforza legacies, or one of turmoil, defined by the shifting tides of power?

Her mother's voice startled her from her thoughts. Silvia Ruffini approached, a shawl draped over her shoulders. "You're out late," Silvia said gently, joining her daughter on the garden path.

"I was thinking about the letter from Father," Costanza admitted. "About what it means for our family."

Silvia nodded, her expression thoughtful. "Your father has weathered many changes in Rome. He will weather this as well. And so will you."

Costanza looked at her mother, her voice tinged with uncertainty. "Do you ever feel… powerless? Watching from afar as the men in our lives shape the world?"

Silvia smiled faintly. "Power comes in many forms, Costanza. You may not sit in the Vatican or lead an army, but you hold power in your wisdom, your influence, and your love. Never doubt that."

The words brought a measure of comfort, and as Costanza returned to the villa, she resolved to face the future with strength. Rome's politics might be turbulent, but her focus remained on her family—the one she had come from and the one she was building. Whatever storms lay ahead, she would meet them with grace and determination.

Chapter 34

The announcement of Clement VII's election to the papacy in 1523 arrived at Santa Fiora in the form of a messenger bearing the Medici seal. For Costanza Farnese, the news brought a mix of curiosity and unease. The Medici name carried a legacy of power and intrigue, and the Farnese family's place in this shifting political landscape suddenly felt more precarious.

Gathered in the villa's solar, Costanza sat with Bosio Sforza, who read the official letter aloud.

"Giulio de' Medici, now Pope Clement VII," he said, his tone thoughtful. "The Medici have always been ambitious, but his election feels like a calculated move by Rome's most powerful families."

Costanza nodded, her hands folded neatly in her lap. "And what does it mean for us? For the Farnese?"

Bosio leaned back, his brow furrowed. "It depends on how Clement chooses to wield his power. He is no stranger to the tensions between the Holy Roman Empire and France. If he aligns with one, the other will retaliate. Rome could become a battlefield, politically or literally."

~

Days later, a letter arrived from Costanza's father, Cardinal Alessandro Farnese, who remained in Rome, navigating the labyrinth of Vatican politics. As she read his words, Costanza felt the weight of the shifting tides more acutely.

Dearest Costanza,

The election of Clement VII has brought both relief and apprehension. He is a capable man, skilled in diplomacy and well-versed in the complexities of Rome's alliances. Yet his Medici blood makes him a target for those who resent their dominance. Already, tensions with the Holy Roman Empire are growing. Charles V expects Clement's loyalty, but the French court whispers promises of mutual benefit. The pope stands at a precipice, and the slightest misstep could send us all into chaos.

Pier Luigi continues to serve our family well, though the political climate grows increasingly volatile. I ask that you remain vigilant in Santa Fiora. While distant from the heart of these

storms, no part of Italy is untouched by their effects.
With love and hope,
Your father,
Alessandro Farnese

That evening, Costanza and Bosio sat by the fire in their private chambers. The warmth of the flames did little to ease the chill of the news they had received.

"This election could change everything," Costanza said, her voice steady but laced with concern. "If Clement aligns with France, Charles V will retaliate. If he sides with the Empire, France will turn on him."

Bosio nodded, his expression serious. "The Medici pope is walking a tightrope. He cannot please both sides, and the Farnese are tied to the Vatican's fortunes. If Rome falters, so do we."

"And my father?" Costanza asked. "He must be under immense pressure."

"He will manage," Bosio assured her. "Alessandro has survived more storms than most. But we must prepare for the possibility that the winds of Rome could reach even Santa Fiora."

As the weeks passed, news of political tensions filtered into Santa Fiora. Rumors swirled of Charles V's displeasure with Clement VII, who had begun to hedge his bets, courting both the French and the Imperial courts. Costanza often found herself in the chapel, seeking solace in prayer as she thought of her father and brothers in Rome.

One afternoon, as she walked the villa grounds with her young son, Guido Ascanio, Costanza found herself reflecting on the fragile balance of power that seemed to govern their lives.

"Your grandfather would tell me to stay strong," she murmured to the boy, who walked beside her, clutching her hand. "And so I will. For you, for our family."

That evening, Costanza penned her own letter to her father, her words a mixture of inquiry and reassurance.

Dearest Father,

Your letter reached me, and as always, your words bring both comfort and clarity. I pray that you remain safe amidst the storms gathering in Rome. The news of Clement VII's election has reached us here, and Bosio and I discuss often what it may mean for the Farnese and the Church as a whole.

I trust your wisdom to guide our family through these uncertain times. Please send word of Pier Luigi and Ranuccio. They are never far from my thoughts, as are you.

Your loving daughter,
Costanza

Distant from Rome, Costanza could feel the reverberations of Clement VII's papacy in her daily life. The Medici pope's decisions would ripple outward, touching every corner of Italy, and Costanza knew the Farnese family must remain vigilant. As she watched the sunset from the villa's terrace that evening, she resolved to face whatever challenges lay ahead with the strength and grace her father had always instilled in her.

For now, the Medici pope ruled Rome, but Costanza could not shake the feeling that the foundations beneath them all were beginning to shift.

Chapter 35

The year 1524 arrived with the chill of uncertainty. For Costanza Sforza, the peace of her life in Santa Fiora stood in sharp contrast to the chaos spreading across Italy. Rumors of battles between French and Imperial forces reached the villa, each tale more alarming than the last. The Italian Wars, which had simmered for years, were now boiling over, threatening to engulf every corner of the peninsula.

One morning, a courier arrived bearing an urgent letter from Costanza's father, Cardinal Alessandro Farnese, whose presence in Rome placed him at the epicenter of these turbulent events. She sat in the villa's library as Bosio opened the missive, reading it aloud.

Dearest Costanza,

The peace we have known is slipping further from our grasp. The French, under King Francis I, have resumed their campaign to reclaim Milan, clashing with the forces of Emperor Charles V. Their battles disrupt the fragile stability of Italy, and the Church is caught in the crossfire of ambition and power.

The Farnese family remains secure for now, but only through careful maneuvering. I have aligned myself with key figures in the papal court, ensuring our interests are protected amidst the shifting alliances. Pier Luigi continues his duties, proving himself both capable and loyal, though these times test even the most steadfast among us.

I urge you to remain cautious. Santa Fiora, while distant from the battles, is not immune to the ripple effects of war. Should tensions escalate further, we must be prepared for what may come.

With love and resolve,
Your father,
Alessandro Farnese

Costanza took the letter and placed it on the table, her hands trembling slightly. The weight of her father's words was clear—this was no passing storm. Italy was in the throes of chaos, and even the Farnese family's influence might not be enough to shield them.

Later that evening, Costanza and Bosio sat in the study, maps of Italy spread across the table between them. Bosio traced a line with his finger, pointing to the territories contested by France and the Holy Roman Empire.

"Milan is the prize," he said. "The French see it as their right, while Charles V will not relinquish it without a fight. Every state caught between them is suffering."

"And Rome?" Costanza asked, her voice tinged with worry.

Bosio leaned back, his brow furrowed. "The Church is playing a dangerous game. Clement VII tries to maintain a delicate balance, but alliances are shifting too quickly. Your father is right—these battles will not stay confined to the north."

Costanza sighed, her gaze fixed on the map. "Do you think Santa Fiora is at risk?"

Bosio met her eyes. "Not directly, but the instability could spread. Bandits, displaced soldiers, even opportunists seeking to exploit the chaos—all could pose a threat. We must ensure the estate is well-protected."

As days turned into weeks, Costanza found herself spending more time in prayer. She thought of her father, maneuvering through the treacherous currents of Vatican politics, and of her brother Pier Luigi, who, despite his fiery nature, had taken on greater responsibilities within the family.

Her thoughts often turned to her young son, Guido Ascanio, now a curious toddler with his father's dark eyes. She watched him play in the gardens, his laughter a balm against the growing unease in her heart.

"What kind of world are we bringing him into?" she asked Bosio one evening as they walked the villa grounds.

Bosio placed a reassuring hand on her shoulder. "A world shaped by our strength and resolve. Whatever storms come, we will weather them together."

By 1525, the news became grimmer. The Battle of Pavia, fought in February, resulted in a decisive Imperial victory. Francis I of France was captured, and his ambitions in Italy were crushed for the moment. This victory for Charles V sent shockwaves through Europe, shifting alliances once more.

Costanza received another letter from her father, his words both cautious and triumphant.

The French suffered a great defeat, and their king was now a prisoner of the emperor. For the moment, the tide turns in favor of the Empire, and Rome breathes a little easier. Yet I urge you to remain vigilant. The balance of power is fragile, and peace, if it comes, will not last long.

She read the letter aloud to Bosio that evening, her voice steady despite the turmoil she felt inside.

"The emperor's victory should bring stability," Bosio said, though his tone carried doubt. "But it may also embolden him to exert more control over the Italian states. Rome's independence could be at risk."

"And the Church?" Costanza asked.

Bosio shook his head. "The Church will be forced to choose its alliances carefully. Your father's skill will be tested more than ever."

As the year drew to a close, Costanza found solace in the resilience of her family. The Farnese name had weathered many storms, and she believed they would endure this one as well. Yet the uncertainty lingered, a reminder that in the ever-changing tides of Italian politics, nothing could be taken for granted.

Standing on the villa's terrace one evening, Costanza gazed out at the distant hills. The future felt as vast and unknowable as the night sky, but she resolved to face it with the same strength that had carried her through every challenge thus far.

"We will endure," she whispered to herself. "We always have."

Chapter 36

The spring of 1527 dawned with an eerie calm. Santa Fiora, nestled in the Tuscan hills, felt far removed from the growing tensions in Rome, yet the undercurrents of unease reached even Costanza's ears. She sat in the nursery, cradling her newest addition to her family, a daughter barely a few months old. Her eldest, Guido, walked beside her, talking happily as he pushed a carved wooden horse across the stone floor to one of his other siblings.

The peaceful scene was shattered by the arrival of a breathless messenger bearing a sealed letter from her father, Cardinal Alessandro Farnese. Costanza's hands trembled as she broke the seal, her heart sinking with every word.

Dearest Costanza,

Rome has fallen into chaos. On the sixth day of May, imperial troops stormed the city, their fury unleashed upon its people. Churches desecrated, treasures looted, homes burned—the Holy City is unrecognizable. His Holiness, Pope Clement VII, has taken refuge in the Castel Sant'Angelo, but his safety is far from assured.

I write to you from a monastery on the outskirts of the city, where I have sought temporary refuge. By God's mercy, I am unharmed, but my heart is heavy with grief for what has been lost. Many of my colleagues were not so fortunate, and the Farnese properties within Rome have suffered greatly.

My dearest daughter, remain in Santa Fiora. The turmoil here is far from over, and the Italian states are in no position to offer stability. Protect your family and pray for Rome.

With love,
Your father,
Alessandro Farnese

Costanza lowered the letter, her mind racing. The Sack of Rome—a catastrophe so unimaginable that it seemed almost unreal—had devastated the very heart of the Church and the city she still considered home.

Bosio entered the room moments later, his brow furrowed as he saw her expression. "What is it?" he asked.

She handed him the letter silently, her voice catching in her throat. As he read, his lips pressed into a grim line.

"This is worse than I feared," he said, folding the letter and setting it on the table. "If Rome has fallen, the Church itself is in jeopardy."

Costanza looked down at her daughter, now asleep in her arms. "What kind of world are we raising them in, Bosio? Guido, our daughter— they deserve peace, not a life overshadowed by war and destruction."

"We will do everything in our power to protect them," Bosio said firmly, kneeling beside her. "The chaos will not reach Santa Fiora. I will see to that."

In the days that followed, more letters arrived from Rome, each one painting a grimmer picture. The imperial troops, mercenaries underpaid and undisciplined, had unleashed terror upon the city. Nobles fled to the countryside, their estates ransacked. Priests and nuns were not spared the violence, and even sacred sites like St. Peter's Basilica were desecrated.

Alessandro Farnese remained in hiding, using his influence to aid those he could, though his resources were stretched thin. Costanza felt a deep pang of guilt for being safe in Santa Fiora while her father endured such suffering. Yet she knew her place was here, protecting her children and supporting Bosio in securing their estate.

One evening, as the villa's servants lit the lanterns, Costanza sat with Bosio in their private chambers. The children were asleep, their soft breaths a faint melody in the quiet of the night.

"I've been thinking about my father," she said, her voice steady but tinged with sadness. "I cannot imagine what it must be like for him—to see Rome in ruins, to know the Church is so vulnerable."

Bosio poured her a goblet of wine and handed it to her. "Your father has always been a survivor, Costanza. He has endured worse storms than this."

She nodded, sipping the wine. "And yet, this feels different. Rome is more than just a city—it is the heart of everything we've built. If it falls, what remains?"

Bosio reached for her hand, his grip firm. "What remains is us. Our family, our strength. Rome will recover, just as we will endure. But for now, we focus on what we can control."

Costanza looked at him, her heart swelling with gratitude. "You're right. The Farnese have always risen from the ashes, and we will again."

In the weeks that followed, Costanza channeled her worry into action. She worked alongside Bosio to ensure Santa Fiora was fortified against any potential unrest, directing resources to secure the estate's borders and protect its people. At the same time, she wrote regularly to her father, offering words of encouragement and updates on her growing family.

Her daughter, whom she named Lucrezia, became a source of light. The infant's laughter and bright eyes reminded Costanza that life continues. Guido and Francesca, too, brought joy with their endless curiosity and mischief, a testament to the resilience of youth.

Though the immediate threat had passed, the Sack of Rome left an indelible mark on Costanza. She carried the weight of her father's experiences, the sorrow of a city brought to its knees, and the knowledge that the world her children would inherit was far from certain.

As she stood on the villa's terrace one evening, the distant hills bathed in the soft glow of twilight, she whispered a prayer for Rome, for her family, and for the strength to face whatever lay ahead.

"We will endure," she murmured, the words both a promise and a challenge. "For them. For all of us."

Chapter 37

The year 1528 brought an uneasy calm to Italy.

The scars of the Sack of Rome were still fresh, and while Pope Clement VII struggled to reassert his authority, whispers of rebellion, alliances, and betrayal rippled through the Italian states. For Costanza Farnese, life at Santa Fiora had settled into a rhythm, though the tension in the air remained palpable.

One crisp morning, Costanza sat in the villa's study with a letter from her father, Cardinal Alessandro Farnese, laid out before her. Bosio, seated beside her, frowned as he read its contents.

Dearest Costanza,
The tides of power are shifting once again.
France and the Empire teeter on the brink of
renewed conflict, and the Church's role hangs in

a precarious balance. The Medici pope, ever cautious, seeks alliances that may prove dangerous for families like ours.

There is talk of a new council to address the corruption within the Church, but this has only stoked tensions among the cardinals. Even here, in Rome, alliances are fracturing. Pier Luigi has asked for my counsel on a matter I cannot detail in writing, but I sense danger. Stay vigilant, my daughter, for what happens here will ripple outward.

With all my love,
Your father,
Alessandro Farnese

Bosio leaned back, his expression grim. "Your father does not write lightly. If he senses danger, we must be prepared."

Costanza nodded, her hand instinctively resting on the letter. "Pier Luigi is involved. Whatever this is, it must be serious."

Days later, a carriage bearing the Farnese crest arrived at Santa Fiora. Pier Luigi, now a hardened figure, stepped out, his presence commanding. Time had only sharpened his features and his air of authority. Costanza greeted him with an embrace, though the tension in his frame was unmistakable.

"Pier Luigi," she said, studying his face. "What brings you here?"

"A warning," he replied, his voice low. "And a favor."

Over dinner, Pier Luigi revealed the crux of his visit. "The Emperor and the Pope are playing a dangerous game. Clement is seeking to strengthen his ties with France, but Charles V will not take kindly to this. The Farnese name has weathered many storms, but we may be caught in the crossfire if the Pope's schemes unravel."

"And what favor do you ask?" Bosio inquired, his tone measured.

Pier Luigi hesitated, his gaze flickering to Costanza. "I need a place to hide certain… documents. Letters and agreements that, if discovered, could destroy not only me but our father as well."

Bosio stiffened. "You bring danger to Santa Fiora."

"I bring survival," Pier Luigi countered. "If these papers fall into the wrong hands, the Farnese name will be dragged into ruin."

Costanza placed a hand on Bosio's arm. "We cannot abandon my father or Pier Luigi. If we are to protect our family, we must act."

After a tense pause, Bosio nodded reluctantly. "Very well. But we must be cautious."

Under the cover of night, Pier Luigi and Bosio worked to hide the documents in an old wine cellar beneath the villa. The air was damp and heavy with the scent of aged oak barrels as the two men sealed the letters in a small, iron-bound chest.

"These letters tie Clement directly to secret negotiations with France," Pier Luigi said. "If Charles discovers them, the Pope's position—and ours—will be compromised."

Bosio looked at him sharply. "You're playing a dangerous game."

"We all are," Pier Luigi replied. "It's the only game we've ever known."

Days later, word reached Santa Fiora that imperial envoys were searching estates across Tuscany, looking for evidence of treachery against Charles V. Costanza's heart raced as the news spread through the villa.

That evening, Pier Luigi and Bosio argued heatedly in the study.

"You've brought them to our doorstep!" Bosio said, his voice barely controlled. "If they search this villa—"

"They won't," Pier Luigi interrupted. "I've taken precautions. The cache is hidden well enough. They'll find nothing."

"And if they do?" Bosio pressed.

Costanza stepped between them, her voice calm but firm. "Enough. We must stay united. Pier Luigi, you'll remain out of sight. Bosio, you'll ensure the staff says nothing of his presence."

Her authority silenced them, and for a moment, she felt the weight of her position—

Countessa of Santa Fiora, protector of the Farnese name.

Two days later, the imperial envoys arrived. Their leader, a severe man in a dark doublet, demanded to speak with Bosio.

"We have reason to believe treasonous correspondence may be hidden within this estate," the man said, his gaze cold.

"You're welcome to search, though you'll find nothing of the sort," Bosio replied smoothly.

Costanza stood nearby, her expression composed. As the soldiers moved through the villa, her heart pounded in her chest, but she betrayed no fear. Guido toddled into the room, clutching a toy horse, and Costanza scooped him into her arms, her smile serene.

"Will these men be staying for dinner, my lord?" she asked Bosio lightly, her voice a perfect mask of innocence.

The leader glanced at her, his suspicion wavering. "That won't be necessary."

The search yielded nothing, and the envoys departed, their frustration evident. As the last soldier left, Costanza exhaled, her knees nearly buckling from the tension.

That night, Pier Luigi prepared to leave Santa Fiora, the documents safely hidden. He clasped Costanza's hand tightly. "You've saved us all tonight."

"You owe me more than thanks," she replied, her voice steady. "You owe me a promise that the Farnese name will survive this chaos."

"It will," he said, his tone resolute. "Because of you."

As he disappeared into the night, Costanza turned to Bosio. "This won't be the last storm we face."

"No," Bosio agreed, wrapping an arm around her. "But together, we'll weather it."

In the quiet of the villa, Costanza gazed at the stars, her resolve hardening. The Farnese family was more than its name—it was its people, its bonds, and its strength. No matter the dangers ahead, she would protect it with everything she had.

Chapter 38

The years between 1528 and 1533 were fraught with shifting alliances, military campaigns, and political upheavals that rippled across Italy. For Costanza, nestled in the relative calm of Santa Fiora, the weight of these changes still pressed heavily on her family. Letters from her father, Cardinal Alessandro Farnese, painted vivid pictures of a world in turmoil—a world where the Farnese name was both a shield and a target.

The Siege of Naples (1528)

In early 1528, news arrived of the French army's siege of Naples. Costanza was in the nursery, overseeing her children's care, when Bosio entered with a letter bearing the crest of the Farnese family.

"The French have launched a siege," he said, handing her the parchment. "Your father writes of chaos in Naples."

Costanza read the letter quickly, her brows knitting together. "The Holy Roman Empire will not let this stand. Charles V won't allow the French to hold Naples."

Bosio nodded. "True. But until the siege ends, the Italian states remain divided. It's a dangerous time for all of us."

The Battle of Landriano (1529)

By June 1529, the siege had failed, and the Battle of Landriano ended in a decisive Imperial victory. Bosio returned from a meeting with local nobles, bringing news of the defeat.

"The French have withdrawn," he told Costanza. "Charles V has won a major victory, and with it, his influence over Italy grows stronger."

Costanza's thoughts immediately turned to her father. "And Rome? How does Clement VII respond?"

Bosio shrugged. "The Pope must tread carefully. He can't afford to alienate Charles, not with the Church still recovering from the Sack of Rome."

The Treaty of Cambrai (August 1529)

Weeks later, the Treaty of Cambrai—known as the Ladies' Peace—was signed. Costanza sat with Bosio in the villa's library, reading her father's latest letter.

"The treaty has brought a fragile peace to Italy. France has withdrawn its claim to Milan, and Charles now holds sway over much of the peninsula. Yet this peace is precarious, built on concessions that may not hold for long."

Costanza set the letter down, her fingers tracing the Farnese crest. "Peace is never truly peace, is it?"

Bosio smiled faintly. "Not in Italy. It's more of a pause—a chance for everyone to catch their breath before the next battle."

Charles V's Coronation (1530)

The news of Charles V's coronation as Holy Roman Emperor in February 1530 arrived with much fanfare. The event marked the last time a pope crowned an emperor, a symbolic gesture of the Church's influence over secular power.

At dinner that evening, Bosio recounted the event for their guests. "Clement VII traveled to Bologna for the coronation," he said. "It was a display of power on both sides. Charles was crowned emperor, but everyone knows the Medici pope has his own agenda."

Costanza listened intently, her gaze steady. "And what of Florence? Has Clement made any progress there?"

Bosio nodded. "He's working to restore Medici rule. The siege of Florence continues, but it won't be long before the city falls."

The Medici's Return to Florence (1530)

By late 1530, Florence had surrendered, and Medici power was restored under Clement VII. For Costanza, the news was bittersweet.

"It's a victory for the Pope," she said to Bosio as they walked through the gardens. "But at what cost? The people of Florence will resent Medici rule, and resentment always festers."

Bosio looked at her thoughtfully. "You sound like your father. Always thinking two steps ahead."

Costanza smiled faintly. "Perhaps I've learned from the best."

A Marriage Alliance (1533)

By 1533, Pope Clement VII was focused on strengthening the Church's ties with France. The marriage of his niece, Catherine de' Medici, to Henry, Duke of Orléans, was both a personal and political triumph.

Costanza received a letter from her father detailing the event.

"The marriage of Catherine de' Medici to the French Duke is a coup for the papacy. Clement VII has secured a powerful ally in France, though the cost of such an alliance remains to be

seen. The Medici name rises once again, but with it comes the shadow of ambition and envy."

Costanza read the letter aloud to Bosio that evening. "The Medici play a dangerous game," she said. "Aligning with France may anger Charles V."

Bosio agreed. "And yet Clement has little choice. The Church is weaker now than ever. He needs France as much as France needs him."

Religious Tensions and a King's Defiance

The final lines of her father's letter hinted at an even greater conflict brewing.

"King Henry VIII of England grows impatient. His demands for an annulment have been denied, and his frustration with the papacy mounts. Clement must tread carefully, for this defiance could fracture the Church itself."

Costanza set the letter down, her expression grim. "The Church cannot afford another schism."

Bosio poured them each a goblet of wine. "No, but if Henry breaks from Rome, it will weaken Clement's position even further."

Costanza raised her glass, her mind swirling with thoughts of the future. "To strength," she said softly. "The only thing that keeps us standing in times like these."

As the years passed, Costanza's understanding of politics deepened. The alliances, betrayals, and battles of Italy were not just stories—they were the very fabric of her family's survival. Each letter from her father reminded her that the Farnese name was both a blessing and a burden, tied inexorably to the fate of Italy and the Church.

Yet in the quiet moments at Santa Fiora, with her children playing at her feet and Bosio by her side, Costanza found strength in the bonds of her own family. No matter how turbulent the world became, she resolved to protect what mattered most.

Chapter 39

The crisp autumn air of October 1534 carried the scent of wood smoke, mingling with the murmurs of anticipation that filled the crowd gathered in St. Peter's Square. Costanza stood near the edge of the throng, her heart pounding as she gazed at the chimney atop the Sistine Chapel. Around her, the city of Rome buzzed with speculation. A conclave had been convened to choose a new pope, and now, the crowd waited for the plume of smoke that would signal the decision.

"Black or white?" whispered Pier Luigi, standing beside her. The second eldest of the Farnese siblings, his usually brash demeanor was subdued today, his eyes fixed on the same chimney.

"White," Costanza replied, her voice steady despite the nerves tightening her chest. "It must be."

Her younger brother, Ranuccio, now a rising figure in the Church, stood on her other side, his crimson cardinal's robes a stark contrast to the plain cloak she wore. "If Father is chosen," he said softly, "It will change everything—for all of us."

Costanza glanced at him, her thoughts swirling. The idea of her father, Cardinal Alessandro Farnese, becoming pope was both thrilling and terrifying. What would it mean for their family? For her?

The crowd erupted into cheers as a plume of white smoke billowed from the chimney, stark against the clear blue sky. The signal was unmistakable: a new pope had been chosen. Costanza's breath caught as she turned to her brothers, their faces reflecting the same mixture of awe and disbelief.

"It's him," Pier Luigi murmured, a rare note of emotion in his voice.

Moments later, a voice rang out from the balcony of St. Peter's Basilica, announcing the name of the new pope: Cardinal Alessandro Farnese, now Pope Paul III.

Costanza felt tears sting her eyes as the crowd roared its approval. Her father, once a young man with little claim to greatness, had ascended to the pinnacle of the Church.

That evening, the Farnese family gathered in a private chamber of the Vatican, the atmosphere electric with celebration. Alessandro, now dressed in the white robes of the papacy, embraced each of his children in turn.

"My dear Costanza," he said, his voice warm as he took her hands in his. "You've always been my strength, my anchor. This moment belongs to all of us."

Costanza smiled, though her mind raced. What would this new role mean for him—for their family? "You've earned this, Father," she said. "The world will be better for your leadership."

Pier Luigi approached, his usual confidence magnified by the moment. "And the Farnese name will rise higher than ever," he said, clasping his father's shoulder. "This is the beginning of a new era."

Alessandro's gaze turned serious. "It is indeed. But with great power comes great responsibility. We must tread carefully, for many will envy what we've built."

Over the next few days, Rome was transformed by the excitement of Pope Paul III's election. Costanza attended a series of ceremonies, marveling at the grandeur of it all— the gilded halls, the solemn processions, the throngs of people cheering her father's name.

Yet behind the splendor, Costanza saw the weight her father now carried. In private, he spoke of his plans to address the Protestant Reformation, to reform the Church, and convene a council that would bring clarity and strength to Catholicism.

"The world is changing, Costanza," he told her during one of their quieter moments. "The Council of Trent will be my legacy. We must respond to the challenges of the Reformation with courage and wisdom."

"And what of us?" she asked gently. "What will this mean for the family?"

"It means opportunity," he said. "Pier Luigi will secure Parma and Piacenza. Ranuccio will rise higher in the Church. And you, my dear, will always have my trust and support."

As the celebrations carried on, Costanza began to notice a change in her father. The man who once spoke so passionately about his family now seemed consumed by the weight of his new responsibilities. Conversations that had once been warm and personal grew formal and measured, his words laced with the gravity of his new role.

Late one evening, Costanza sought him out in the private apartments of the Vatican. She found him seated at a large wooden desk, poring over letters and documents by the dim light of a single candle.

"Father," she said softly, stepping into the room. "May I join you?"

He glanced up, the weariness in his eyes momentarily replaced by a faint smile. "Always, my dear."

She sat across from him, studying the lines on his face. "Do you ever wish things had turned out differently?"

He leaned back in his chair, his expression thoughtful. "Every path comes with its sacrifices, Costanza. To serve the Church at this level means leaving behind certain comforts—certain freedoms. But I do not regret it. This is where I am meant to be."

"And what of us?" she asked quietly. "Your family?"

His gaze softened, but there was a hint of distance in his eyes. "You are all my heart, but my duty is now to a greater family—the Church, the faithful. I hope you can understand that."

Costanza nodded, though a part of her ached at the subtle finality in his tone. "I do, Father. But promise me one thing."

"What is that?" he asked, leaning forward.

"That no matter how high you rise, you will never forget the roots of our family. We are part of you, just as you are part of us."

He reached across the desk, taking her hands in his. "That, my dear, is a promise I can make."

As she left his chambers, Costanza couldn't shake the feeling that their family was changing, the ties that bound them stretched by the gravity of her father's new role. Yet his words lingered, offering a fragile comfort: they were still Farnese, bound by blood and legacy, even in the shadow of the papacy.

Chapter 40

The Ruffini villa was unusually quiet when the messenger arrived, his dusty boots and solemn expression betraying the significance of his news. Silvia Ruffini, seated by the window with her embroidery, looked up sharply as the servant entered with a letter bearing the papal seal. Though she had anticipated this moment for years, the sight of the letter made her chest tighten.

She dismissed the servant with a nod, unfolding the parchment with steady hands. Her eyes scanned the familiar handwriting of her former lover, Alessandro Farnese, now Pope Paul III.

Silvia,
The weight of the papacy rests heavily upon me.
The Church demands my full devotion, leaving

little room for the bonds that once defined my life. I write this with a heavy heart, knowing that my responsibilities to God and the faithful require sacrifices I never imagined. You and the children remain my greatest love, but my path has diverged irrevocably from yours.

Take solace in the knowledge that our family's name will rise to heights few could dream of. I will do all in my power to secure the futures of our children. This, I promise you.

Alessandro

Silvia lowered the letter, her composure unbroken, though a storm raged within her. The man she had shared so much of her life with was now lost to her in all but name. Though their love had long been shrouded in discretion, it had been real, tangible. And now, even that was slipping away.

That evening, Silvia gathered her children in the villa's courtyard. Pier Luigi, always the defiant one, paced restlessly, while Costanza sat with quiet dignity, her hands folded in her lap. Ranuccio, still young and impressionable, leaned against his sister, sensing the tension but not fully understanding its depth.

"Your father has ascended to the highest position in the Church," Silvia began, her voice calm but firm. "He is now Pope Paul III, a man whose life belongs not to us but to God and the Church."

Pier Luigi stopped pacing, his expression a mix of pride and frustration. "So he abandons us for Rome? For the Church?"

Silvia's gaze sharpened. "Do not mistake duty for abandonment, Pier Luigi. This is a path he has chosen and one that elevates all of us. But yes, it comes with sacrifices—sacrifices we must also bear."

Costanza spoke softly, her tone measured. "He has not forgotten us. He wrote that his work will secure our futures."

"And what of now?" Pier Luigi challenged. "What of the years he spent building this legacy while we waited in the shadows?"

Silvia's lips pressed into a thin line. "Your father has always been a man of ambition, and his ambition has brought us here—to a place of influence and power few could imagine. But I won't deny that it has cost us. That is why we must stand together now, as a family."

Later that night, Silvia found Costanza sitting in the garden, the soft light of the moon casting a glow over her thoughtful expression.

"You're quiet tonight," Silvia said, taking a seat beside her.

"I was thinking about what this means for all of us," Costanza admitted. "Father's rise is remarkable, but it feels… distant. As if he belongs to the world now, and not to us."

Silvia nodded, her gaze fixed on the roses blooming nearby. "That is the price of greatness, my dear. Alessandro's love for us is real, but his love for the Church will always come first. It is a choice he made long ago."

Costanza looked at her mother, her brow furrowed. "And you? How do you bear it?"

Silvia smiled faintly, though her eyes glistened with unshed tears. "Because I see the bigger picture. Our family is stronger because of his sacrifices. You, Pier Luigi, Ranuccio—you are his legacy. And I am content knowing that I played a part in shaping that legacy."

Costanza reached for her mother's hand, squeezing it gently. "You're stronger than I ever realized."

Silvia turned to her daughter, her smile softening. "And so are you, Costanza. Never forget that."

As the days passed, the Farnese family began to adjust to their new reality. Alessandro's role as pope brought them prestige and security, but it also created a chasm that could never fully be bridged. For Silvia, it was a bittersweet victory. She had always known that Alessandro's ambition would take him far, but she had not anticipated how much it would take from them all.

Still, she found solace in her children and in the knowledge that the Farnese name would endure, rising above the chaos of Italy's politics and the Church's turmoil. And in her quiet moments, she allowed herself to remember the man Alessandro had been before he became

Pope Paul III—a man of passion, ambition, and love.

Chapter 41

The announcement arrived on a crisp autumn morning in 1534, carried by a courier bearing the unmistakable seal of Pope Paul III. Costanza sat in the drawing room of the Santa Fiora villa, the faint scent of grapes drifting in from the open windows. Her husband, Bosio, stood nearby, the sunlight casting a soft glow on his broad shoulders. They had been expecting news from Rome, but this letter carried weight beyond mere correspondence.

With steady hands, Costanza broke the seal and began to read. Her eyes moved over the elegant script, and as the words sank in, she felt her breath catch.

"Guido, son" she said, her voice tinged with both awe and disbelief. "You've been named Cardinal-Deacon of Santa Fiora."

Her son looked up from the chessboard where he had been deep in thought, his brow furrowing slightly. "Cardinal?" he echoed, the word foreign and vast on his tongue.

Bosio moved to her side, reading over her shoulder. A slow, proud smile spread across his face. "Our son, a cardinal," he said, placing a hand on Guido's shoulder. "This is no ordinary honor. It is a declaration of the Farnese legacy."

Guido, ever composed beyond his years, straightened his back. "Aren't I too young," he said, his voice steady but uncertain. "How can I fulfill such a role?"

Costanza knelt before him, taking his hands in hers. "You carry the blood of Farnese and Sforza, Guido. Your grandfather, the Pope himself, sees your potential. This is more than a title—it is a responsibility, and he believes you are ready."

The following days were filled with preparation. Guido's tutors doubled their efforts, teaching him the intricacies of Church law, diplomacy, and theology. Costanza watched her son closely, pride warring with apprehension. While Guido possessed a natural intelligence and a calm demeanor, she worried about the weight such a position would place on his young shoulders.

One evening, she found him in the library, surrounded by books and scrolls. He looked up as she entered, his expression thoughtful. "Mother," he began, "What does it mean to be a cardinal? Truly?"

Costanza sat beside him, her gaze softening. "It means you are a shepherd to the faithful, a steward of the Church's power and its people. But it also means you must navigate a world of politics, ambition, and intrigue. Your grandfather has given you a great honor, but it comes with equal responsibility."

Guido nodded slowly. "I want to make him proud. And you."

"You already have," Costanza said, brushing a lock of dark hair from his forehead. "But remember, Guido, you are more than your title. You are my son. That will never change."

The family departed for Rome to present Guido formally at the Vatican. The journey was filled with a sense of purpose, their retinue reflecting the importance of the occasion. Costanza and Bosio rode in a carriage, while Guido traveled in another, flanked by attendants. The sight of the Eternal City's skyline filled Costanza's heart with a mix of nostalgia and trepidation. Rome, with all its grandeur and shadows, was a place where ambition thrived and innocence often faded.

At the Vatican, Pope Paul III greeted them personally. Guido knelt before his grandfather, who placed a hand on his head in a gesture of both blessing and authority. "You carry the Sforza name into the Church," the Pope said, his voice solemn. "It is a name of strength, but also of duty. Serve with wisdom, Guido. The eyes of the world are upon you."

The investiture ceremony was a spectacle of grandeur, attended by cardinals, nobility, and dignitaries from across Europe. Guido, clad in the crimson robes of a cardinal, stood with quiet dignity. As the symbols of his office were bestowed upon him, Costanza felt tears prick her eyes. Her son, once a boy playing in the gardens of Santa Fiora, now stood among the most powerful men in Christendom.

When the ceremony concluded, Guido approached his mother and father, his expression calm but his eyes shining with determination. "I will not fail you," he said simply.

Costanza embraced him tightly. "You are already more than I could have hoped for."

In the weeks that followed, Guido assumed his duties with a focus that belied his youth. He attended meetings, managed benefices, and began to learn the intricacies of Church administration. While many questioned the appointment of someone so young, Guido's composure and intelligence quickly silenced his critics.

Costanza watched him from the sidelines, her pride tempered by a mother's eternal concern. She knew the path ahead would not be easy, but she also knew Guido was uniquely prepared for it. As she returned to Santa Fiora, she carried with her the image of her son standing tall in the halls of the Vatican—a symbol of both the

Farnese family's legacy and the enduring bond between mother and child.

Chapter 42

That year brought a renewed sense of purpose to Rome, as whispers of artistic genius and monumental projects spread through its bustling streets. For Costanza Sforza, the daughter of the newly elected Pope Paul III, the election of her father had already set a whirlwind of change in motion. Yet, among the many transformations unfolding in the Eternal City, one name captured the attention of all: Michelangelo Buonarroti.

Costanza stood on the balcony of the Farnese Palace, her gaze drawn to the distant dome of St. Peter's Basilica. The sprawling construction site had long symbolized both the Church's aspirations and its challenges. Now, under her father's papacy, it was poised to become a masterpiece that would define Rome for centuries.

"Michelangelo has arrived," Bosio said, joining her with a letter in hand. "He has left Florence for good and taken up residence in Rome."

Costanza turned, her curiosity piqued. "The sculptor of David and the painter of the Sistine Chapel ceiling? He is to work for Father?"

Bosio nodded, handing her the parchment. "Father intends to entrust him with the greatest tasks of the Church. Michelangelo is to shape the very image of the papacy."

As Costanza read the letter, she felt a thrill of anticipation. Her father's ambitions were unrelenting, but this—this was something extraordinary. Through Michelangelo's genius, Pope Paul III's legacy would be carved not only in marble but into the heart of history itself.

~

The first audience between Pope Paul III and Michelangelo was a moment steeped in both reverence and practicality. Alessandro Farnese, now adorned in the white robes of the papacy, welcomed the artist into the Vatican with an air of cordiality.

"You are no stranger to Rome, Michelangelo," Paul III said, gesturing for the artist to sit. "But under my papacy, your work will find new purpose. The Church needs your vision, your skill. Will you give it to us?"

Michelangelo, a man of few words and boundless talent, bowed his head slightly. "Your

Holiness, I serve the divine through my craft. If it is God's will, I shall serve the Church."

The pope's smile was warm but calculating. "Indeed, it is God's will—and mine. St. Peter's must be completed, not merely as a symbol of faith, but as a beacon of our strength. You will transform it, Michelangelo."

The artist's reluctance was evident, but he could not refuse the pope's command. For Michelangelo, the commission was both a burden and an honor. The Basilica was a vast, unfinished canvas, its potential overshadowed by decades of delays and conflicting visions. Now, the responsibility of its completion rested on his shoulders.

~

In 1535, Pope Paul III formally appointed Michelangelo as the chief architect of St. Peter's Basilica, a decision that sent ripples through the corridors of the Vatican and beyond. The artist's bold ideas clashed with those of his predecessor, Antonio da Sangallo the Younger, whose elaborate plans had left the structure burdened by complexity.

Michelangelo envisioned a simpler, more harmonious design—a Greek-cross layout crowned by a dome that would pierce the heavens. His approach was revolutionary, stripping away unnecessary ornamentation to reveal the raw power of form and proportion.

Costanza overheard her father discussing the project with a group of cardinals one evening. She lingered in the shadows, her curiosity outweighing the propriety of eavesdropping.

"Michelangelo is a genius," her father said, his tone resolute. "But genius must be guided. His designs will elevate St. Peter's to a place beyond mortal comprehension."

"And the costs?" one of the cardinals asked.

Paul III's voice grew sharper. "This is not a question of cost. It is a question of legacy. What is money compared to the eternal glory of the Church?"

Costanza smiled to herself, her admiration for her father growing. His vision was unyielding, and through Michelangelo, that vision would take shape.

~

As the months passed, the work on St. Peter's Basilica progressed under Michelangelo's direction. Letters from the Vatican detailed the artist's dedication and the challenges he faced in reimagining the grand structure.

One evening, Costanza sat with Bosio in the garden of their villa in Santa Fiora. Their children nearby, their laughter a soothing counterpoint to the weighty topics on their minds.

"Do you think Michelangelo will succeed?" Costanza asked, her gaze fixed on the horizon.

Bosio considered her question carefully. "If anyone can, it is Michelangelo. But such greatness often comes at a cost—to the artist, to the patrons, to those who follow."

Costanza nodded, her thoughts turning to her father. "He has always been willing to pay the cost. Sometimes, I wonder if we, his family, are part of that price."

Bosio reached for her hand, his grip reassuring. "Your father's ambitions are vast, Costanza, but so is his love for you. Remember that."

~

By the end of 1535, Michelangelo had begun to leave his mark on St. Peter's Basilica, though the road ahead was long and fraught with challenges. For Costanza, the artist's presence in Rome was a symbol of her father's determination to reshape not only the Church but the world itself.

As she walked through the halls of the Farnese Palace, she felt a surge of pride. The Farnese name was no longer just a mark of power—it was a beacon of creativity, faith, and resilience. And in the hands of Michelangelo, that legacy would endure.

Chapter 43

The silence of the Sistine Chapel was profound, broken only by the faint echo of footsteps as Michelangelo Buonarroti walked the length of the sacred space. The air was cool and still, heavy with the weight of centuries of worship and the grandeur of the frescoes above him. Yet his eyes were not drawn upward to his own earlier work on the ceiling, but forward—to the altar wall, bare and waiting.

Michelangelo paused before the vast expanse of plaster, his hand brushing the rough surface. It was here that Pope Paul III had commanded him to create something extraordinary. Something that would capture the power of divine justice, the authority of the Church, and the salvation—or damnation—of every soul.

"You must make them see eternity," the Pope had said, his voice filled with fervor. "Show them the glory of Christ's return and the weight of their judgment."

Michelangelo had nodded, but words felt inadequate for such a monumental task. How could one encapsulate the infinite in the confines of a wall? Yet as he stood there now, the first faint stirrings of a vision began to take shape.

He closed his eyes, and in the darkness of his mind, the wall came alive. At its center stood Christ, radiant and commanding, his arm raised in judgment. Around him, the heavens churned with angels and saints, their forms both ethereal and solid. Michelangelo could see the Virgin Mary beside Christ, her posture humble yet full of grace, her gaze turned away as if unable to bear the weight of the scene.

Below, the earth erupted with chaos and movement. The saved ascended in rapturous ecstasy, their bodies reaching toward the light. The damned, twisted in agony, were dragged downward by demons, their faces etched with terror and despair.

Michelangelo's heart raced as the vision sharpened. He could see the folds of fabric, the tension in muscles, the expressions of awe and fear. The colors seemed to glow in his mind's eye—deep blues for the heavens, fiery reds and oranges for the damned, and golden hues for the divine.

He opened his eyes, his breath coming quickly. The wall before him was blank once more, but he could already see the finished work overlaying its surface, as vivid as if it had already been painted.

The day the commission was finalized, Michelangelo sat with Pope Paul III in a private chamber of the Vatican. The Pope, resplendent in his white robes, leaned forward with an intensity that made even the great artist uneasy.

"You understand what I ask of you," the Pope said. "This is not merely art—it is a testament to the power of the Church, a message to the faithful and the wayward alike. They must look upon it and see the weight of their choices, the eternal consequences of sin and virtue."

Michelangelo nodded, his hands folded tightly in his lap. "I will do as you ask, Holy Father. But such a work… it will take time."

"Take the time you need," Paul III replied. "For this fresco will stand as a legacy of faith, one that will outlast us all."

The next day, Michelangelo sat in his studio, sketching the figures that had burned themselves into his mind during his vision in the chapel. His charcoal moved swiftly over the parchment, bringing to life the forms of Christ, Mary, the angels, and the damned. Yet for every line he drew, a hundred questions emerged.

How should the light fall on Christ's figure? Should his expression be one of stern judgment or quiet compassion? How could the movements of the saved convey both their joy and their desperation to reach the divine?

Frustration crept in as the sketches piled up around him. Michelangelo tossed one to the floor, then another. He rested his head in his hands, the enormity of the task weighing on him.

It was then that a quiet knock sounded at the door. A messenger from the Vatican entered, carrying a letter sealed with the papal crest. Michelangelo broke the seal and read the brief note.

"Your work will remind the world of its place before God," it said in the Pope's hand. *"Do not strive for perfection, for it is unattainable. Strive for truth."*

The words struck him deeply. Truth. That was the key. This fresco was not about creating beauty or perfection—it was about capturing the essence of humanity's relationship with the divine.

The day Michelangelo applied the first brushstroke to the wall, the Sistine Chapel was empty, save for a handful of his assistants and the quiet presence of Pope Paul III. The Pope watched silently as the artist climbed the scaffolding, his movements deliberate and steady.

As the brush met the plaster, Michelangelo felt a strange calm wash over him. This was the beginning of something greater than himself, a work that would speak to the souls of countless generations.

Hours turned into days, and days into weeks. Slowly, the figures of the fresco began to emerge, their forms shaped by the master's hand and the fire of his vision. Christ, the Virgin, the saints, and the damned took their places on the wall, each stroke a testament to Michelangelo's relentless pursuit of truth.

~

Costanza Farnese, visiting the Vatican with her husband during the early stages of the fresco's creation, stood in awe beneath the towering scaffold. She craned her neck to see the faint outlines of the work taking shape above.

"Your father's choice of Michelangelo was wise," Bosio said, standing beside her. "This will be a masterpiece, a reflection of his papacy's strength."

Costanza nodded, her gaze never leaving the wall. "It's more than a masterpiece," she murmured. "It's a reminder of what we all face—judgment, redemption, eternity."

As she walked through the chapel, her thoughts lingered on the fresco, on the vision that Michelangelo was bringing to life. It was a work that would define her father's papacy and serve as a powerful reminder of the Church's authority and the fragility of the human soul.

Chapter 44

1535

The soft light of dawn filtered through the windows of the Sforza villa in Santa Fiora, painting the walls with a golden hue. Costanza stood by the window, gazing out at the dewy hills below. A letter from Rome rested on the table behind her, its contents already read and reread.

"Archbishop of Naples," Costanza murmured, the weight of the words settling over her like a fine mist. Her nephew Ranuccio, barely fourteen years old, had been appointed to one of the most prestigious ecclesiastical positions in the Church. It was both a triumph for the family and a sobering reminder of the Farnese entanglement with power.

Bosio entered the room, his steady presence grounding her. "You've been quiet since the letter arrived," he said, crossing the room to stand beside her. "What troubles you?"

She looked at him, her expression a mixture of pride and unease. "It's Ranuccio. He's a boy, Bosio. And now he's been given the weight of an archbishopric. How can someone so young bear such a burden?"

Bosio smiled faintly, placing a reassuring hand on her shoulder. "Ranuccio is a Farnese. If anyone can rise to the occasion, it's him. And he has your father's guidance."

"Guidance, yes," she sighed, her gaze drifting back to the hills beyond the villa. "But also expectations. Father sees this as another move in his grand design, another piece in his legacy. What if it's too much for Ranuccio?"

Bosio's hand slipped down to hers, intertwining their fingers. "Then he has you. You've always been the one to steady your family, to remind them of who they are."

She nodded slowly, drawing strength from his words. "Perhaps. But I can't help but worry. The Church is no easy path, especially for a child thrust into its power games."

Bosio's expression turned thoughtful. "It's not. But he will have allies—and your father is no stranger to the pressures of leadership. Ranuccio will learn, Costanza. And one day, he may look back on this as the foundation of his strength."

Costanza remained quiet, her thoughts lingering on her nephew. The Church, for all its splendor, was an arena of ambition and politics. For Ranuccio, it would be both a test and a crucible.

That afternoon, Costanza read the letter again, this time aloud to her eldest son, now a curious and bright-eyed five-year-old.

"'Ranuccio has been appointed Archbishop of Naples,'" she read, her voice steady. "'His Holiness believes this is a fitting role for one of his lineage, a step toward securing our family's influence in the Church.'"

Her son frowned slightly. "Does cousin Ranuccio have to leave Rome?"

"Yes, my love," she said, smoothing his hair. "He will live in Naples now, where he will learn to serve God and the Church."

"Will he visit us?" the boy asked, his voice tinged with concern.

"I hope so," she replied, kissing his forehead. "But his path is different now, and we must pray for his success."

Later that evening, as the villa settled into a quiet lull, Costanza penned her own letter to Ranuccio. Her words were careful, balancing her pride with the concern of a concerned aunt.

My dearest nephew,

The news of your appointment has filled me with pride. To see you rise so high at such a young age is a testament to your strength and our family's legacy. Yet, I would be remiss if I did not remind you that with this great honor comes great responsibility.

You will face challenges, Ranuccio. The Church is as much a battlefield as any army, and you must navigate it with wisdom and grace. Lean on your grandfather's guidance, but trust your own heart as well. Remember the lessons of your childhood: loyalty, humility, and strength.

You are young, yes, but you are also capable. Do not let anyone tell you otherwise.

With all my love,

Aunt Costanza

A week later, Costanza stood at her brother's villa's entrance as Ranuccio prepared to leave for Naples. Dressed in crimson robes that seemed to swallow his slender frame, he looked both dignified and vulnerable. His youthful face betrayed his nervousness, though he tried to hide it behind a composed expression.

"You'll write to me, won't you?" Costanza asked, pulling him into a gentle embrace.

"Of course, aunty," Ranuccio replied, his voice steady but tinged with emotion. "I'll need your advice more than ever."

She smiled, placing a hand on his cheek. "And you'll have it, always."

As his carriage disappeared down the road, Costanza stood there for a long while, her heart heavy yet hopeful. Her nephew was stepping into a world far removed from his quiet home, a world of power and intrigue that would test him in ways she could hardly imagine.

But she believed in him. He was a Farnese, after all. And if anyone could rise to the occasion, it was Ranuccio.

Chapter 45

The end of the summer of 1535 arrived with its usual warmth, the Tuscan hills bathed in golden light. But for Costanza Farnese, Countessa of Santa Fiora, the season would forever be marked by sorrow. Word of Bosio Sforza's illness had reached her late, and by the time she returned from visiting her family in Rome, it was clear that the end was near.

Costanza entered the bedchamber where Bosio lay, the room dimly lit and heavy with the scent of herbs. His once-strong frame was frail, his skin pale against the crisp linen sheets. Yet when his eyes met hers, they still held the warmth and strength she had fallen in love with.

"My love," he rasped, his voice weak but steady. "You're here."

She knelt beside him, taking his hand in hers. "My love."

For a long moment, they simply looked at one another, the silence between them filled with unspoken words. Costanza's tears threatened to fall, but she blinked them back, determined to be strong for him.

"You've been the best part of my life, Costanza," Bosio said softly. "And I need you to promise me something."

"Anything," she whispered, her voice trembling.

"Stay strong. For our children. For yourself. Santa Fiora will need you, and so will they."

"I will," she vowed, her hand tightening around his. "I promise."

Bosio managed a faint smile, his eyes closing as if the effort of speaking had drained him. "You are my everything."

He passed away later that night, his final breath leaving the room in a stillness that felt eternal. Costanza remained by his side, her grief a quiet storm that raged within her.

The funeral was a solemn affair, attended by nobles, clergy, and the people of Santa Fiora, who had come to pay their respects to a man they deeply admired. As the procession wound through the streets, Costanza walked at its center, her black veil concealing the tears that would not stop falling.

Since her eldest son, Guido, now seventeen and firmly established in his role as a Cardinal, the responsibility of inheriting the Sforza legacy fell upon Mario, the next in line to carry the family name. He stood by her side, his small frame trembling as he clung to her hand. His wide, tear-filled eyes searched hers for answers. "What happens now, Mother?" he asked, his voice fragile and uncertain, barely rising above the solemn tolling of bells.

Costanza placed a steadying hand on her five-year-old's shoulder. "We carry on. For your father. For our family."

In the following weeks, Costanza found herself navigating a world that felt familiar and alien. Without Bosio, the villa seemed emptier, and the days were longer. She threw herself into her duties, overseeing the estate and ensuring her children were cared for. But in the quiet moments, the weight of her loss threatened to consume her.

One evening, she found herself alone in the gardens Bosio had loved so much. The air carried the earthy fragrance of the Tuscan hills, mingled with the faint scent of wild thyme and sun-warmed stone, a bittersweet reminder of the life they had built together. She sank to her knees by the fountain, her composure finally breaking.

"How do I do this without you?" she whispered to the night, her tears falling freely.

Over time, Costanza began to find a new strength within herself. Bosio's death had left a void, but it had also ignited a resolve she had not known she possessed. She became more involved in the affairs of Santa Fiora, ensuring that the Sforza name remained strong and respected. Her children became her anchor, their laughter and presence a balm for her grief.

Letters from her father, Pope Paul III, provided comfort and encouragement. *"You have always been strong, my daughter,"* he wrote. *"Bosio's loss is a heavy burden, but I know you will rise to meet it. You are Farnese, and that strength runs through your veins."*

Bosio's death marked a profound turning point in Costanza's life. No longer just a wife or a mother, she had become the leader of her family, the matriarch who would safeguard the Sforza legacy. The responsibilities that lay ahead were daunting, but she faced them with the same unwavering resolve that had defined her life.

She found solace in the quiet sanctuary of the chapel near the family's burial site. Shaded by cypress trees that whispered in the wind, the burial ground offered a refuge from the burdens of her new role. The scent of wild thyme and sun-warmed earth mingled with the solemn stillness as she knelt by Bosio's grave, her hand resting gently on the cool stone marker bearing his name.

"I will honor you," she whispered, her voice steady despite the ache in her heart. "And I will make sure our children remember the man you were—the strength you gave, the love you left behind."

The wind carried her words across the tranquil landscape, blending with the faint tolling of distant bells. In this sacred space, surrounded by the land they had built their life upon, she felt his presence. It was as if the very earth echoed with the steadfastness that had defined him.

Here, by his grave, Costanza allowed herself to grieve and to gather strength. She spoke to him often, her words a quiet vow to carry forward the legacy they had created together. In those moments, she was not alone; the love they had shared lingered, guiding her through the uncertain days to come.

Chapter 46

1537

The crisp morning air carried the scent of pine and wildflowers through the hills of Santa Fiora, but for Costanza Farnese, there was no solace in the beauty of her surroundings. The past two years had brought a cascade of challenges that threatened to unmoor her carefully built world.

Bosio was gone—his steadying presence ripped from her life when death claimed him unexpectedly in 1535. Costanza had been thrust into a role she had never anticipated, not only the matriarch of the Sforza household but also the sole guardian of its legacy. For all her strength, it was a heavy mantle to bear.

Santa Fiora itself had begun to unravel in Bosio's absence. The local nobility questioned the leadership of her son, young Mario, now the Count of Santa Fiora. Though Mario was eager to prove himself, he was just a child, far too young to wield power in a world where men hungered for it like wolves. The council of advisors Bosio had left behind proved more interested in enriching themselves than preserving the Sforza name.

Costanza took it upon herself to protect her son's inheritance, navigating the murky waters of politics and feudal governance with a resolve that surprised even her. She sat at the head of council meetings, her black mourning gown a stark reminder of her authority. Her voice, sharp and unyielding, cut through the posturing of the councilors who dared to underestimate her.

"Santa Fiora does not belong to you," she told them one afternoon, her gaze as cold as the stone walls of the villa's great hall. "It belongs to my son. And I will not see it squandered by greed or incompetence."

The men fell silent, but their sullen faces told her the battle was far from over.

Beyond the villa, the land itself was under siege. Banditry had surged in the wake of Bosio's death, as word of Santa Fiora's vulnerabilities spread. Small villages within their territory reported stolen livestock, raided granaries, and homes burned to the ground. Costanza dispatched armed guards to patrol the roads, but the men's loyalty was tenuous at best.

One evening, a messenger arrived from a nearby hamlet, his face pale with fear. "They came at dusk," he stammered, his hands trembling as he held out a blood-stained cloth. "Took everything. Said the Sforza can't protect us anymore."

Costanza felt her chest tighten as she took the cloth—a child's tunic, torn and smeared with mud. The implication was clear: if she couldn't control the lands, her family's reputation would crumble, and the fragile alliances that kept Santa Fiora afloat.

Desperate times called for desperate measures. Against the advice of her council, Costanza rode out with a small escort to confront the leader of the bandits—a man known only as Falco. The journey through the wooded hills was fraught with danger, but Costanza's resolve never wavered.

When they reached the bandits' camp, Falco emerged from the shadows, a tall figure with a scar slashing across his face. He laughed as she dismounted her horse. "I expected a Sforza boy, not a Sforza woman."

"You should know better than to underestimate a Farnese," Costanza retorted, her voice cutting through the murmurs of his men. "You seek to challenge our rule? Let me tell you what that truly means."

Falco's grin faltered slightly, but before he could reply, one of his men stepped forward hesitantly. A wiry man with a thin, angular face, he leaned toward Falco, whispering loudly enough for others to hear. "Do you know who she is?" he hissed. "That's Costanza Farnese, daughter of Pope Paul III. Her family doesn't just rule lands—they command armies. The Vatican's warriors answer to her father. She could bring God's wrath down upon us."

Falco's expression darkened as the words sank in, his scarred face tightening with tension. His gaze flicked back to Costanza, studying her anew, as though weighing the truth of the man's claim against her composed yet fiery demeanor.

Costanza seized the moment, stepping closer, her eyes burning with fury. "You've made your point," she continued, her tone icy and unyielding. "But let me make mine clear, if you continue to threaten these lands, I will see you hang from the highest tree. And if you think you can hide from justice, remember who my father is and the forces he commands. There is nowhere you could go where his reach would not find you."

The camp fell silent, the weight of her words pressing down on the bandits like a storm cloud. Murmurs rippled through the gathered men, and a few shifted uneasily, casting nervous glances at one another.

After what felt like an eternity, Falco inclined his head, a flicker of respect and calculation in his eyes. "You've got fire, my lady," he said. "But fire can burn."

"We'll see who burns," Costanza replied sharply before turning on her heels.

As she mounted her horse, she allowed herself a small smile, her presence lingering like a shadow over the camp. Within days, the bandits dispersed, their attacks ceasing as suddenly as they had begun. Whispers of "the Farnese woman's wrath" traveled across the hills, ensuring that no other group dared to challenge her lands again.

Yet even as she quelled the external threats, the weight of her family's future bore down on her. Mario's education became her top priority. She worked tirelessly with tutors to ensure he would grow into a ruler worthy of the Sforza name, even as whispers of discontent among the nobles reached her ears.

Her daughters, Francesca and Giulia, were growing into young women, and Costanza knew their futures would be tied to advantageous marriages. She wrote letters to her father, Pope Paul III, seeking his guidance and support, but his replies were often terse, preoccupied with the political maneuverings of Rome.

One night, as she tucked Mario into bed, he looked up at her with wide, questioning eyes. "Will Father ever come back?" he asked.

Costanza's throat tightened, but she forced a gentle smile. "No, my love," she said softly. "But he watches over us, always."

As Mario drifted to sleep, Costanza sat by his bedside, her hand resting on his small one. In the quiet of the night, the weight of her responsibilities felt almost unbearable. Yet she knew she had no choice but to carry on—for her children, for her family, for the legacy Bosio had left behind.

By the end of 1537, the tides had begun to turn. The banditry had ceased, and the local nobility, while still wary of her authority, had come to respect her resolve. Costanza had proven herself not just as a widow or a mother but as a leader capable of weathering the storms that threatened to engulf her family.

And yet, she knew the peace was fragile. The world outside Santa Fiora was changing, and the Farnese name was both a shield and a target. As she stood on the balcony of the villa one evening, gazing out at the rolling hills, Costanza allowed herself a rare moment of vulnerability.

"I will protect them," she whispered to the night. "No matter the cost."

In the distance, the bells of the chapel tolled softly, a reminder of the faith that had always guided her. As the first stars began to appear in the darkening sky, Costanza resolved to face whatever came next with the same unyielding strength that had carried her through the darkest days.

Chapter 47

The year 1537 marked a turning point for Pier Luigi Farnese, whose ambitions were as fiery as his temperament. With his father, Pope Paul III, now firmly entrenched as the head of the Catholic Church, Pier Luigi saw an opportunity to secure not only his place within the Farnese legacy but also a lasting dominion of his own.

His role as commander-in-chief of the papal forces afforded him access to the corridors of power, and he wielded his authority with a confidence that bordered on audacity. For Pier Luigi, this was not merely about loyalty to his father—it was about carving his name into the annals of history.

At the Farnese Palace, tensions simmered as Pier Luigi pushed relentlessly for titles and land. Costanza, visiting Rome with her children found herself caught in the crossfire of her brother's ambitions.

"You're pressing him too hard," she said one evening as they walked through the grand hall. "Father has given you much already—your position in the army, his trust. Why demand more?"

Pier Luigi scoffed, his pace quickening. "Because trust isn't enough, Costanza. The Farnese name must have roots—real roots. Land, titles, power. Otherwise, we're just pawns in someone else's game."

"And you think Father doesn't see that?" she countered. "He's the Pope, Pier Luigi. He understands the stakes better than anyone."

He stopped abruptly, turning to face her. "Then he should act like it. The Medici have Florence, and the Sforza have Milan. What do we have? A legacy built on promises?"

Costanza's gaze softened, though her voice remained firm. "We have each other. And Father's rise has secured more for us than you realize. Be patient."

Pier Luigi shook his head, a bitter smile playing at his lips. "Patience is for those who lack ambition. I'll make him see reason."

Pier Luigi's persistence paid off. In 1537, Pope Paul III granted him the Duchy of Castro, a territory carved from papal lands in northern Lazio. The move was strategic, solidifying Farnese influence in the region while rewarding Pier Luigi for his service to the Church.

The formal investiture ceremony was a grand affair, held in Rome with all the pomp befitting such an occasion. Costanza attended with her oldest daughter, Francesca, and her expression was a mixture of pride and unease as she watched her brother accept the title.

"Do you think this will satisfy him?" Francesca murmured as they sat among the assembled nobility.

"For a time," Costanza replied, her gaze fixed on Pier Luigi's triumphant figure. "But ambition is a fire. The more it's fed, the more it consumes."

As Pier Luigi stepped forward to receive the symbols of his new office, he caught Costanza's eye and offered her a faint smile. For a brief moment, she saw the boy he had once been— fiery, determined, and unyielding. But that boy was now a man, and his ambitions were no longer confined to dreams.

The creation of the Duchy of Castro marked a new era for the Farnese family. With Pier Luigi installed as Duke, the Farnese name carried greater weight in the Italian political landscape. Yet the move was not without controversy. Other noble families bristled at the sudden rise of the Farnese, viewing Pier Luigi's new title as an overreach of papal authority.

Back in Santa Fiora, Costanza received a letter from her father, now Pope Paul III, explaining his decision.

"Costanza, my dear, the duchy is as much a safeguard for our family as it is a reward for Pier Luigi. In these times, land is security, and Castro will anchor our legacy for generations to come. Yet I worry. Ambition is a double-edged sword, and I fear Pier Luigi's drive may outpace his caution. Watch over him, my daughter, for his sake and ours."

Late that night, Costanza stood on her Tuscany villa's balcony, the letter still clutched in her hand. The moonlight illuminated the rolling hills of Santa Fiora, a world far removed from the political games of Rome. Yet even here, the consequences of her family's actions reverberated.

Francesca joined her, wrapping a cloak around her shoulders. "You're thinking about Pier Luigi."

"I am," she admitted. "Your Grandfather's words are true. Pier Luigi's ambition is both his strength and his weakness."

Francesca nodded. "The duchy is a victory, but it will attract enemies. You know that as well as I do."

Costanza sighed, leaning against the balustrade. "I only hope it doesn't cost us more than it's worth."

As the Farnese name continued to rise, so too did the stakes. Pier Luigi, now Duke of Castro, had achieved his goal, but the path he walked was fraught with peril. For Costanza, the moment was bittersweet—a triumph for her brother, but a reminder of the fragile balance her family had to maintain in the volatile world of Renaissance Italy.

Chapter 48

1538

The warm Tuscan sun bathed the hills of Santa Fiora as Costanza sat in the shaded courtyard of the villa, a letter in her hands. The seal of her father, Pope Paul III, glinted in the light, its significance as weighty as the words it carried. She smoothed the parchment, taking a deep breath before reading aloud to her older children, who lounged nearby under the pergola.

"My dearest daughter,
The Lord has seen fit to bless us with a moment of peace. With great effort and perseverance, I have mediated a truce between Emperor Charles V and King Francis of France. The Truce of Nice, as it will be known, is not without its fragility, but it offers respite from the flames of war. Pray that this peace holds, for it is as

delicate as the petals of a rose and as easily torn. "

Costanza paused, her voice catching on the weight of the words. "He's done it," she said softly, lowering the letter. "Father has brought peace—for now."

Giulia, now a poised young woman, leaned forward, her expression thoughtful. "It's no small feat to bring two such men to the table, let alone to an agreement. But I wonder—at what cost?"

Costanza met her gaze, her brow furrowed. "What do you mean?"

"The Church's role as a mediator gives it immense power," Giulia explained, echoing lessons she had likely gleaned from her brother Guido. "But it also places a target on its back. Charles and Francis may have signed this truce, but their ambitions haven't diminished. Grandfather's position becomes more precarious with each entanglement."

Costanza nodded, her fingers brushing the edge of the letter. "He must know that. And yet, he takes the risk. For what? For peace? For the Farnese name?"

"For both, perhaps," Giulia replied. "Grandfather is a man of vision. He sees the Church as more than a spiritual guide—it is a force capable of shaping the fate of nations. But that vision comes with enemies."

That evening, Costanza sat by the fire, the letter resting on her lap as she stared into the flames. The flickering light cast long shadows across the room, mirroring the doubts in her mind.

"What are you thinking?" Francesca, her eldest daughter, asked, settling beside her mother.

"That I should be proud," Costanza admitted. "And I am. But I also worry. Grandfather's ambition has always been a double-edged sword. For every step forward, there is a cost. For every peace he brokers, there are those who would see him fail."

Francesca reached for her hand, her grip warm and steady. "He's not alone, Mother. He has us, Uncle Ranuccio, and the strength of the Farnese name."

"But strength invites challenge," Costanza murmured, her gaze distant. "I fear what might come next."

The following morning, Costanza made her way to the small chapel on the estate. The air inside was cool and quiet, the faint scent of wax lingering from the candles that burned softly on the altar. Kneeling before the crucifix, she clasped her hands together, her thoughts a tangled web of pride and concern.

"Lord, guide him," she whispered, her voice trembling. "Give him the wisdom to navigate this path, the strength to endure its trials, and the grace to remember why he chose it."

At the edge of the chapel, Costanza paused to touch Bosio's headstone, a gesture that had become part of her daily routine. The family burial site, shaded by towering cypress trees, exuded a serene stillness. The scent of wild thyme filled the air as she knelt by the grave.

"I will honor you," she murmured, tracing the engraved letters of his name. Her voice was steady, though her heart ached with the void his absence had left. "And I will make sure our children remember the man you were—the strength you gave, the love you left behind."

As she rose, a sense of calm washed over her. Her father's path was his own, but it was one that carried the weight of their entire family. She could not walk it for him, but she could pray— and she could prepare.

Later that day, Costanza, Francesca, and Giulia walked through the gardens, the letter from Pope Paul III tucked securely into her pocket. The late afternoon sun painted the landscape in hues of gold and green, a stark contrast to the tensions brewing beyond the hills of Santa Fiora.

"Do you think the truce will hold?" Giulia asked, breaking the silence.

Costanza hesitated before replying. "For a time, perhaps. However, Charles and Francis are not men who settle for less than dominance. This is a pause, not an end."

"And the Church?" Giulia pressed. "What does this mean for Grandfather?"

"It means he has positioned himself as a bridge between empires," Costanza said. "But bridges are vulnerable. They carry the weight of the world while standing on fragile foundations."

Francesca stopped, turning to face her mother. "Then what do we do?"

"We prepare," Costanza said simply. "We strengthen our own position. Your Grandfather's actions ripple outward, but here, in Santa Fiora, we must remain steady. For our future."

Francesca nodded, her resolve hardening. The Truce of Nice was a triumph, but it was also a reminder of the delicate balance her family walked. The Farnese name carried power, but it also carried risk. And in the ever-shifting world of Renaissance Italy, survival required more than ambition—it required vigilance.

As the sun dipped below the horizon, Costanza gazed out at the hills from the chapel's edge. Her hand rested on Bosio's headstone, her gaze fixed on the horizon. Whatever came next, she would face it with the strength and grace her father had taught her. For the Farnese name. For her family. For herself.

Chapter 49

1538

The Farnese Palace in Rome buzzed with preparation as Vittoria Farnese, the eldest daughter of Pier Luigi Farnese and Gerolama Orsini, prepared to marry Guidobaldo II della Rovere, Duke of Urbino. The match was a triumph of diplomacy, weaving the Farnese family into the intricate tapestry of Italian noble alliances. For Vittoria, however, it marked the beginning of a new chapter, one filled with duty, expectations, and the weight of her family's ambitions.

Costanza arrived in Rome with her children, her heart both heavy and light. The city had always been a mix of home and battlefield, a place where the Farnese name was both celebrated and scrutinized. As she stepped into the grand hall of the palace, memories of her own introduction to noble society flooded her mind. Yet today was not about her; it was about her niece, stepping into the same world that Costanza had long since learned to navigate.

The morning of the wedding dawned bright and clear, the crisp autumn air invigorating the bustling city. Costanza found Vittoria in her chambers, surrounded by attendants who worked to perfect every detail of her appearance. The bride's gown, a masterpiece of gold and ivory silk, shimmered as she moved, and her dark hair was adorned with pearls and a delicate veil.

"You look stunning," Costanza said warmly, stepping forward to embrace her niece.

Vittoria smiled faintly, though her eyes betrayed her nerves. "Thank you, Aunt Costanza. I only hope I can fulfill the expectations this union brings."

"You will," Costanza assured her. "You've always carried yourself with grace and strength. This is no different."

Vittoria's gaze softened. "And you? Do you ever miss the simplicity of Santa Fiora?"

Costanza chuckled. "Every day. But life is rarely simple for us, Vittoria. We must make peace with the complexity."

The ceremony was held at the Basilica of Santa Maria in Aracoeli, its grandeur befitting the union of two powerful houses. Costanza sat near the front with Bosio and her children, her heart swelling with pride as Vittoria walked down the aisle. Guidobaldo, resplendent in a doublet of deep blue velvet embroidered with the della Rovere family crest, awaited his bride at the altar.

The vows were exchanged under the watchful eyes of cardinals and nobles, the air heavy with the significance of the moment. For the Farnese family, this marriage was more than a personal union—it was a political statement, a testament to their growing influence.

As Vittoria and Guidobaldo turned to face the congregation, the applause that erupted felt like a wave of approval for the Farnese name itself. Costanza clapped along with the others, though her mind drifted to the reality of what lay ahead for Vittoria—a life dictated by duty, alliances, and the expectations of her new family.

Later that evening, as the celebrations unfolded in the Farnese Palace, Costanza found Vittoria alone on a balcony overlooking the city. The soft glow of lanterns illuminated her features, and for a moment, she looked every bit the noblewoman she was now expected to be.

"Stealing a moment to yourself?" Costanza asked gently, joining her.

Vittoria nodded. "It's overwhelming, isn't it? To know that every step I take now reflects not just on me, but on the Farnese name."

Costanza placed a reassuring hand on her niece's arm. "It is overwhelming, yes. But you are not alone. You carry the strength of our family with you, and that is no small thing.”

Vittoria turned to her, her expression wistful. “You speak as though you’ve made peace with it. Have you?”

Costanza hesitated, her gaze drifting to the distant lights of Rome. “I’ve learned to carry it, Vittoria. And so will you.”

Chapter 50

The warm afternoon light of Santa Fiora filtered through the open window as Costanza sat at her writing desk, a rare moment of quiet amid her duties. A servant entered the room, carrying a sealed letter on a silver tray.

"A letter for you, Countessa," he announced, bowing slightly.

Costanza's heart skipped as she recognized the seal of the della Rovere family. Carefully, she broke the wax and unfolded the parchment. The handwriting was unmistakable—elegant yet hurried, reflecting the vibrant personality of her niece, Vittoria.

My Dearest Aunt Costanza,
I hope this letter finds you well and surrounded by the serenity of Santa Fiora. I write to you from Urbino, where the rolling hills

seem to cradle the city like a precious gem. It is a place of breathtaking beauty and unending activity, and though I have only been here a short time, I feel as if I have stepped into an entirely different world.

The court of Urbino, under Guidobaldo, is a hub of brilliance and ambition. The Della Rovere name, as you know, carries immense weight, and their legacy is one steeped in both power and culture. It is said that Pope Julius II himself, the great "Warrior Pope," envisioned Urbino as the embodiment of Renaissance ideals. Walking these halls, I can feel his presence in the grandeur around me.

Everywhere I turn, there is art. The walls of the palace are adorned with frescoes, and the library overflows with ancient manuscripts. Guidobaldo takes great pride in this collection, often inviting scholars and philosophers to discuss their works at length. They speak of Plato and Aristotle as if they were old friends, and I, though eager to listen, find myself somewhat daunted by their intellectual fervor.

I must tell you about a visit to the palace gallery. There, I stood before a portrait by Raphael, painted years ago during his time here as a young man. His brush captured the essence of Urbino's court with such perfection that it almost brought tears to my eyes. To live surrounded by such beauty is both a privilege and a responsibility, for one cannot help but feel the weight of history pressing upon them.

Guidobaldo, my husband, is a man of quiet determination. His focus is unwavering, and his vision for the future of Urbino is clear. He often speaks of his grandfather, Pope Julius II, and the legacy he left behind. "It is not enough to inherit power," he tells me. "We must shape it into something greater."

Yet, with this ambition comes tension. The delicate balance of alliances between the Italian states keeps him awake many nights. The Medici in Florence, the Farnese in Rome, the d'Este in Ferrara—all jockey for influence, and Guidobaldo navigates this web with precision. I see now how much of our lives are dictated by the whims of politics, though I do my best to remind him of the human side of power.

At times, I feel like an outsider, though I am treated with great kindness. The della Rovere family carries themselves with a certain aloofness, their pride evident in every gesture. I try to bring warmth to their formality, to remind them that power without grace is brittle. Guidobaldo appreciates my efforts, I think, though he rarely says so in words.

Aunt, do you ever wonder if our lives are our own? I love Guidobaldo for his strength and vision, but I sometimes long for the simplicity of our days in Rome. The Farnese name carries its own burdens, but at least I always felt anchored by family. Here, I am a part of something magnificent, yet I cannot help but feel that I am also alone.

I often think of you, dear Aunt, and the wisdom you have shared with me. Your strength in navigating the complexities of our world inspires me daily. Guidobaldo's court is brilliant, but it is also filled with whispers and hidden motives. I try to follow your example, to listen more than I speak and to observe what others might miss.

How is my grandfather, His Holiness? I hear tales of his reforms and the weight he carries as the head of the Church. And my father, Pier Luigi—does he continue to assert himself in Rome? I know his ambitions sometimes trouble you, but his determination is a reflection of the Farnese spirit, is it not?

One day, I hope you will visit Urbino. I would show you the gallery, the library, and the gardens that overlook the hills. Perhaps you would remind me of what it means to be both Farnese and myself. For now, I remain here, learning, observing, and doing my best to honor both the della Rovere name and our own.

Please write to me soon, Aunt. Your letters are a balm to my soul.

With love and admiration,
Vittoria

Costanza set the letter down, her chest tight with emotion. Vittoria's words carried a longing that resonated deeply. The Farnese name had opened doors for all of them, but it had also placed a weight upon their shoulders that few could bear without struggle.

"Guido," she called softly. Her eldest son appeared in the doorway, his cardinal's robes carefully set aside for the comforts of home, his expression curious and attentive.

"A letter from Aunt Vittoria?" he asked, noting the parchment in her hands.

"She writes of Urbino," Costanza replied, gazing out the window toward the horizon. "And of the balance we all strive for—between duty and self."

Guido stepped closer, his presence as steadying as his words. "She has you as an example, Mother. If anyone can guide her through the challenges of our name, it is you."

Costanza smiled faintly, folding the letter. "I hope so. For the Farnese name, it may be a gift, but it is also a burden. And she carries it with dignity."

Guido rested a hand on his mother's shoulder, his tone calm yet sincere. "You've shown us all how to bear that burden. Aunt Vittoria will find her way, just as you have."

As the light faded from the room, Costanza resolved to write back to Vittoria, offering words of encouragement and wisdom. For in this family of power and ambition, their bond as women—and as a family—was a strength that would endure.

Chapter 51

1538

The Farnese Palace was once again a flurry of activity as preparations began for another significant union—this time, the marriage of Ottavio Farnese, Vittoria's younger brother, to Margaret of Austria, the illegitimate daughter of Emperor Charles V. The match was an even greater triumph, solidifying ties between the Farnese family and the Holy Roman Empire.

Costanza received the invitation with mixed emotions. The political implications of the marriage were undeniable, but it also served as a reminder of the sacrifices required to uphold their family's legacy. As she and her children made the journey to Bologna for the wedding, she couldn't help but reflect on the contrast between her own marriage, rooted in love, and the calculated alliances her family often pursued.

The wedding ceremony took place in Bologna, chosen for its neutrality and significance as the site of Charles V's coronation. Margaret, resplendent in a gown of crimson and gold, exuded the poise of someone well-versed in the politics of her lineage. Ottavio, though young, carried himself with a confidence that belied his years.

As Costanza watched the ceremony, she couldn't help but feel a pang of sympathy for Margaret. Like Vittoria, Margaret was stepping into a world where personal desires often took a backseat to political strategy.

During the reception, Costanza found herself seated near members of Charles V's court. The tension was palpable, as alliances forged through marriage were often fragile. She overheard snippets of conversation about the growing power of the Farnese family, some voices admiring, others skeptical.

Later in the evening, Costanza approached Ottavio, who stood near the edge of the hall, observing the festivities.

"Congratulations, dear nephew," she said warmly. "You've done the family proud."

Ottavio smiled faintly. "Thank you, Aunt Costanza. Though I fear I am still learning the art of diplomacy."

"You'll learn," she assured him. "But remember, Ottavio, this is more than an alliance.

Margaret is your partner now. Treat her as such, and you'll find strength in each other."

He nodded thoughtfully. "I'll try. But it's daunting, isn't it? To carry the expectations of so many."

Costanza placed a hand on his arm. "It is. But you are a Farnese, and we were born to meet those expectations. Trust yourself."

As Costanza and her children prepared to return to Santa Fiora, she couldn't help but feel the weight of what her family had accomplished. The marriages of Vittoria and Ottavio had secured alliances that would shape the future of Italy, but they had also highlighted the sacrifices required to achieve such power.

Sitting by the window of their carriage, Costanza watched the rolling hills pass by, her thoughts heavy with the knowledge that the Farnese name, for all its grandeur, was built on the delicate balance of love and duty.

For her siblings and their children, those scales tilted heavily toward duty. For her, they had found an equilibrium, but it was a balance she never took for granted.

Chapter 52

The summer sun of 1540 cast a golden glow over the hills of Santa Fiora, but Costanza's mind was far from the peaceful scenery surrounding her home. A letter from Rome rested on her writing desk, the seal of Pope Paul III unmistakable. Its contents were heavy with significance, revealing the weight of her father's latest achievements.

Costanza sat in the shaded courtyard of the villa, the soft laughter of her younger children echoing faintly from the garden. She reread the letter, her lips pressing together as she took in its most significant announcement: the formal approval of the Society of Jesus, a bold new order dedicated to defending the Church.

Later, with the letter tucked in her hand, she made her way to the family burial site near the chapel. The site was shaded by towering olive trees, their stillness mirroring her solemn mood. Kneeling beside Bosio's grave, she placed the letter gently on the carved stone that bore his name.

"They've done it, Bosio," she murmured, her fingers brushing the edge of the marker. "The Jesuits—Father's vision for reform—is becoming real. A new order, with education and missionary work at its heart." She paused, her voice softening. "But the risks, Bosio. I wonder if Father truly sees them."

The stillness of the burial ground felt almost alive, the quiet presence of Bosio's memory steadying her as she continued. "Ignatius of Loyola, his men—they're loyal to the Church, fearless even. But their boldness will put them in the crosshairs of every enemy Father already faces. And Father—he thrives on this, doesn't he? Balancing empires, confronting kings, and now placing faith in this new order."

The wind rustled through the olive trees as if carrying her words. "You would have known what to say, Bosio. You always did. You'd remind me to have faith, to see the strength in him, in all of us."

A messenger had arrived earlier with another letter, bringing news of her brother Pier Luigi. As commander-in-chief of the papal forces and Duke of Castro, his role in their father's plans was growing ever more pivotal. The conflict between Emperor Charles V and King Francis I simmered just below the surface, and Pier Luigi stood at the center of the delicate truce brokered by the Farnese name.

Costanza's thoughts turned to her children as she knelt by the grave, her hand lingering on the stone. "What kind of world will they inherit, Bosio? One shaped by their grandfather's ambition and their uncle's sword? Will they be ready for it?"

As dusk settled over Santa Fiora, she rose, brushing her hands against her skirts. The air was thick with the scent of wild thyme and sun-warmed earth, grounding her in the present even as her thoughts lingered on the uncertain future.

Returning to the villa, Costanza gathered her children in the drawing room. Alessandro, now seventeen, listened intently as she read aloud the letter from their grandfather. Mario and Faustina sat close by, their expressions a mix of pride and curiosity.

"Grandfather has approved the Jesuits," she said. "A new order to defend the Church and confront the challenges of these times."

Alessandro, ever perceptive, folded his arms thoughtfully. "A bold move. But one that will invite enemies."

Costanza nodded, her gaze steady. "Yes. And yet, he does not waver. He believes in what he's building."

"And Pier Luigi?" Mario asked. "What role does he play in this?"

"Your uncle wields Father's authority like a sword," Costanza replied, her tone both proud and cautious. "But swords draw attention. We must hope he wields it wisely."

Later that night, Costanza returned to the graveyard, the moonlight casting a soft glow over the cypress trees. Kneeling once more, she placed her hands gently on Bosio's headstone.

"I miss you," she whispered, her voice trembling. "But I will carry this. For our children, for our name. I will carry it all."

The wind stirred, carrying the distant sound of the church bells. In that moment, she felt a quiet strength settle within her. The Farnese name carried weight, but so did she. She would endure, as she always had, for her family and for the legacy they were bound to protect.

Chapter 53

The autumn sun cast a golden glow over the hills of Santa Fiora, but the serenity of the countryside was often disrupted by the letters that arrived from Rome. Costanza Farnese, seated at her writing desk, smoothed out a parchment bearing her father's seal. The words within carried news that, while far from home, felt deeply personal—shaping the legacy of her family and the Church they were so entwined with.

The letter began with a somber account of the Colloquy of Regensburg in 1541. Her father, Pope Paul III, had supported the gathering of Catholic and Protestant leaders, hoping to bridge the chasm that threatened to tear Christendom apart. Yet, as the letter recounted, the talks had ended in failure.

"Doctrinal concessions," her father had written, "Are not the path to unity but to weakness."

Costanza read the words aloud to her children that evening as they sat in their study. He leaned back in his chair, his expression thoughtful. "He's right to hold firm," Alessandro said. "The Church cannot bend to appease dissenters, but this failure will embolden them."

"What does this mean for the future?" Costanza asked, her voice laced with concern.

Alessandro gestured toward the map that hung on the wall—a patchwork of fractured territories across Europe. "It means the divide grows deeper. And when faith is divided, so too is power."

The following year, news of the Roman Inquisition reached Santa Fiora. Pope Paul III had restructured the Inquisition to combat heresy, appointing trusted officials to enforce doctrinal purity. Costanza found herself torn between pride in her father's decisive leadership and unease at the methods being employed.

"I understand the necessity," she confided to Giulia during one of their evening walks in the garden. "But it's a heavy-handed approach. Will it not create more fear than faith?"

Giulia placed a reassuring hand on hers. "Fear is a weapon, Mother. One the Church must wield carefully. Your father knows this better than anyone."

Still, the thought of people being scrutinized, questioned, and condemned unsettled her. In the quiet hours of the night, as her children slept, she prayed not only for her father's strength but also for his compassion.

In 1543, another piece of news reached the Sforza household: the publication of Nicolaus Copernicus' De Revolutionibus Orbium Coelestium. The idea that the Earth revolved around the sun was revolutionary—and controversial. The letter from Rome, penned by one of Costanza's contacts, described the murmurs of unease among the Church's scholars.

"It's fascinating," Costanza said to Francesca as they discussed the work one evening. "The universe, so vast and intricate. How could this not inspire wonder?"

Francesca, ever the pragmatist, shook her head. "Wonder is dangerous when it challenges the authority of the Church. If the heavens do not align with scripture, what else might people begin to question?"

Costanza frowned but said nothing. Her faith was strong, yet she couldn't ignore the allure of new knowledge. It was a tension she felt often— between the traditions of the past and the possibilities of the future.

By 1544, the political landscape of Europe shifted once again with the signing of the Treaty of Crépy. The treaty ended hostilities between

Charles V, Holy Roman Emperor, and Francis I of France, bringing a temporary reprieve to the Italian states.

A letter from her brother Pier Luigi, now Duke of Castro, carried the news. *"Father's role in mediating this peace has strengthened the Church's position,"* he wrote. *"But peace in Italy is as fleeting as spring rains. We must remain vigilant."*

Costanza shared the letter with her children over dinner. "Do you think this peace will last?" she asked.

Mario sipped his wine, considering. "It's a reprieve, nothing more. The rivalry between France and the Empire is like a fire—smothered for now but ready to ignite again."

As Costanza gazed at her children, she wondered what kind of world they would inherit. Her father's papacy had brought prestige to the Farnese name, but it also tied them inexorably to the shifting sands of politics and faith.

Later that evening, Costanza sat alone in the villa's chapel, her thoughts heavy with the weight of the letters she had read. The Colloquy's failure, the Inquisition's rise, the challenge of Copernicus' ideas, and the fragile peace of Crépy all painted a picture of a world in flux.

"Father," she whispered, gazing at the flickering candlelight, "You carry the Church's burdens, but they spill over into our lives as well. I pray for your strength, but I also pray for your wisdom."

In that moment, Costanza realized that while her father's actions reverberated across Europe, they also shaped the intimate fabric of her own family's life. And as much as she admired his resolve, she could not help but fear the costs of his ambition.

Chapter 54

1542

The quiet stillness of the Pauline Chapel enveloped Michelangelo as he stood before its bare walls. The room, modest in size compared to the grandeur of the Sistine Chapel, exuded an intimate solemnity. It was here, Pope Paul III had decreed that he wanted Michelangelo's next masterpiece—a work that would reflect the essence of faith and the trials of the Church's greatest saints.

"The Conversion of Saul," the Pope had said, his voice steady with conviction. "And the Crucifixion of St. Peter. Two moments that define the triumph of faith over doubt, of courage in the face of fear."

Michelangelo nodded, though his mind already raced ahead. He could feel the weight of the Pope's request pressing down on him, the enormity of the stories he was meant to capture.

As the hours turned into days, Michelangelo returned to the chapel often, the empty walls both taunting and inspiring him. On one such visit, he closed his eyes and let his mind drift, allowing the silence to guide his thoughts.

In his vision, the first scene unfolded with vivid clarity. Saul, later known as St. Paul, lay sprawled on the ground, blinded by divine light. Around him, chaos reigned—soldiers and horses scattered, their movements frozen in shock and awe. At the center of it all was the light, blinding and pure, radiating from the heavens as if God Himself had reached down to touch the earth.

Michelangelo could see Saul's face, contorted with fear and revelation, his arms outstretched as though reaching for something he could not yet comprehend. The figures around him were captured mid-motion, their bodies twisted in expressions of terror and confusion. The light dominated the scene, dwarfing the human forms and emphasizing the power of the divine.

His vision shifted, and the second scene emerged. St. Peter, the rock upon which the Church was built, hung upside down on a crude wooden cross. His face, lined with age and suffering, radiated both pain and unyielding faith. Around him, Roman soldiers jeered, their faces twisted with cruelty, yet there was something hauntingly human in their expressions—a glimmer of doubt, perhaps, or the unease of witnessing such unwavering conviction.

The composition was stark and visceral. Peter's twisted body mirrored the brutality of his death, but his upward gaze defied the physical agony, a testament to the spiritual strength that transcended his mortal suffering.

Michelangelo opened his eyes, his breath quickened. The walls of the chapel were still blank, but in his mind, they were alive with movement, light, and emotion.

Weeks later, Michelangelo met with Pope Paul III in a private audience. The Pope, now deeply immersed in the challenges of his papacy, greeted the artist with the same fervor he had shown when commissioning The Last Judgment.

"The Pauline Chapel is not for the masses," the Pope said, his tone quiet but firm. "It is for those who serve God, who seek solace and strength in their devotion. Your work here must speak to the heart of faith, Michelangelo. It must remind us of the trials that test our belief and the grace that sustains us."

Michelangelo inclined his head. "The saints you've chosen, Holy Father—Saul and Peter— they embody the extremes of faith. One found it in a moment of blindness, the other in the face of death."

Paul III smiled faintly. "Then you understand. Make them unforgettable."

Michelangelo's sketches began to take form, his hands moving with a confidence born of inspiration. He worked tirelessly in his studio, refining the lines that would define Saul's dramatic conversion and Peter's final sacrifice. His charcoal strokes captured every detail—the tension in a soldier's arm, the intensity of divine light, the raw agony etched into Peter's face.

As he climbed the scaffolding in the chapel for the first time, Michelangelo felt the familiar surge of purpose. The blank plaster before him no longer intimidated; it beckoned, ready to bear the weight of his vision.

The Conversion of Saul took shape first. Michelangelo's brush brought the scene to life, the interplay of light and shadow drawing the viewer's eye to Saul's prostrate figure. The horses reared in terror, their muscles taut, while the soldiers shielded their eyes from the divine brilliance. The celestial light, painted with layer upon layer of translucent pigment, seemed almost to glow from within, a testament to the artist's genius.

The Crucifixion of St. Peter followed. The saint's inverted form dominated the composition, his weathered face a study in suffering and faith. The soldiers' movements were chaotic yet deliberate, their hands gripping the ropes and nails with brutal precision. Above it all, Peter's gaze reached toward an unseen heaven, a silent declaration of his unshakable belief.

~

During one of her rare trips to Rome, Costanza stood in the Pauline Chapel, her children at her side. The frescoes were nearly complete, their vivid imagery filling the space with a sense of both awe and unease.

"It's magnificent," she murmured to Faustina, who stood quietly beside her. "But it's… unsettling."

Faustina nodded. "Faith is not always comforting, Mother. These frescoes remind us of its cost—the trials, the sacrifices. They are a reflection of the world we live in, as much as the world we hope for."

Costanza's gaze lingered on Peter's upturned face, her thoughts turning to her father and the weight he carried as Pope. "Do you think he sees these trials as his own?"

"I think," Faustina said thoughtfully, "Grandfather believes his faith is what makes him endure them."

As they left the chapel, Costanza cast one last glance at Michelangelo, perched high on the scaffolding, his brush moving with tireless precision. She wondered if the artist, too, saw his work as a test of faith, a way to reconcile the divine with the earthly.

When the frescoes were unveiled, they were met with both admiration and contemplation. The scenes Michelangelo had envisioned now adorned the walls of the Pauline Chapel, their raw emotion and spiritual depth leaving an indelible mark on all who saw them.

For Pope Paul III, the frescoes were a triumph—a testament to the enduring power of faith and the Church's role in guiding the faithful. For Michelangelo, they were another chapter in his relentless pursuit of truth, a reminder that art, like faith, demanded both sacrifice and transcendence.

Chapter 55

1545

The chill of early spring lingered in the air as the news reached Santa Fiora—Ranuccio Farnese, Costanza's young nephew, had been elevated to the rank of cardinal, and Pier Luigi, her brother, was now the Duke of Parma and Piacenza. It was a monumental year for the Farnese family, their influence reaching new heights as Pope Paul III cemented his legacy.

Costanza sat in the family's study, a letter from her father resting on the desk before her. The seal of the papacy was unbroken, but even before she opened it, she knew the contents would carry both pride and caution. Mario knocked before entering the room, his expression thoughtful as he handed her a goblet of wine.

"More news from Rome, Mother?" he asked, settling into the chair beside her.

Costanza nodded, breaking the seal and unfolding the parchment. Her eyes scanned the familiar script of her father's hand.

"To my dearest daughter,
The Farnese name has reached heights I once only dreamed of. Ranuccio has been made a cardinal, a role he will grow into under my guidance. Pier Luigi has been granted the Duchy of Parma and Piacenza, securing our family's foothold in Northern Italy. Yet with these blessings come great responsibilities—and greater risks. The world watches us closely now, Costanza. Pray for your brothers and for me, as the weight of this legacy grows heavier with each passing day.
Your loving father,
Paul III"

She set the letter down, her thoughts churning. "Ranuccio, a cardinal at sixteen. It feels too soon."

Mario leaned forward, his gaze steady. "Grandfather has always understood the power of timing. By elevating Ranuccio now, he strengthens his position in the Church. Youth can be a weapon as much as a vulnerability."

"And Pier Luigi?" Costanza asked, her tone edged with worry. "The Duchy of Parma and Piacenza is a bold move. It will anger many."

Mario sighed. "It's a double-edged sword. Uncle Pier Luigi gains authority, but he will also face opposition—from local lords, from rival families, and even within the Church. Grandfather must believe the benefits outweigh the risks."

In the weeks that followed, letters from Rome described the pageantry of Ranuccio's elevation. Costanza imagined her young nephew dressed in cardinal crimson, his boyish features still bearing traces of the child she remembered. The weight of his new title would undoubtedly transform him, but she hoped the guidance of her father would temper the burdens of such responsibility.

One evening, as she sat by the fire with her children, she shared her thoughts aloud. "I worry for Ranuccio. He's intelligent, but he's still so young. The Church is no place for innocence."

Faustina took her hand, her voice gentle. "He's not alone, Mother. Grandfather will guide him, and the family will protect him. But you're right—the Church is a battlefield, and Ranuccio must learn to fight."

Costanza nodded, her gaze distant. "I just hope he remembers who he is, beyond the robes and titles."

~

The granting of Parma and Piacenza to Pier Luigi was an unprecedented move, signaling Pope Paul III's intent to secure Farnese influence for generations. The duchy, carved from papal territories, was both a gift and a test—a chance for Pier Luigi to prove himself as a ruler, but also a magnet for envy and dissent.

Costanza received letters from Pier Luigi himself, filled with a mix of pride and frustration. *"The people of Parma are cautious,"* he wrote in one letter. *"They see me as an outsider, a symbol of Rome's interference. But they will learn to respect me, if not love me."*

Mario, ever realistic, offered his perspective as they discussed the news. "Pier Luigi will have to rule with both strength and diplomacy. If he leans too heavily on force, he'll risk rebellion. But if he's too lenient, his authority will crumble."

Costanza sighed. "He's always been headstrong. I only hope he listens to my Father's advice."

~

That summer, Costanza sat in the gardens of Santa Fiora. The letters from Rome and Parma had slowed, but their impact lingered in her thoughts. The Farnese family was at the pinnacle of its power, yet she couldn't shake the feeling that they stood on a precipice, the weight of ambition threatening to pull them down.

Giulia joined her, a letter in hand. "News from Rome," she said, passing it to her. "Grandfather writes of the Council of Trent. It begins soon."

Costanza unfolded the letter, her brow furrowing as she read. "Another challenge," she murmured. "As if he doesn't already carry enough."

"He thrives on challenges," Giulia said with a faint smile. "And so do you, Mother."

Costanza looked up at her daughter, her expression softening. "Perhaps. But sometimes I wonder if we ask too much of ourselves—and each other."

Giulia leaned down, pressing a kiss to her mother's forehead. "We endure because we must. And because we believe in what we're building."

As the sun dipped below the hills, casting the gardens in golden light, Costanza resolved to support her family however she could. The Farnese name had brought them power, but it also demanded resilience. And in the face of an uncertain future, she knew that resilience would be their greatest strength.

Chapter 56

The letter arrived on a cold December morning, carried by a courier who wore the solemn expression of one who understood the weight of his message. Costanza sat in the sunlit study of the villa in Santa Fiora, her hands steady as she broke the seal bearing the papal crest. The script inside, penned in her father's distinctive hand, was as resolute as the man himself.

"To my dearest daughter,
Today marks the beginning of a new chapter for the Church and for our family. The Council of Trent convenes under my guidance, its purpose to confront the fractures within our faith and restore the unity of Christendom. Pray for us, Costanza, for this task is as perilous as it is necessary.
Your loving father,
Paul III"

Costanza's hands trembled slightly as she read, the enormity of the moment settling upon her like a cloak. The Council of Trent—she had heard whispers of its importance, discussions between her household and the other nobles, murmurs in the quiet corners of Rome. Now, it was real, and her father stood at its helm.

Later that evening, as the fire crackled in the hearth, Guido explained the significance of the council to the family, aware of the monumental event unfolding far from their Tuscan home.

"The Church has been fractured for decades," Guido began, his tone thoughtful. "The Protestant Reformation has spread like wildfire, challenging the very foundations of Rome's authority. Our Grandfather's council is an attempt to stem the tide, to reaffirm Catholic doctrine, and address the corruption that allowed the schism to take root."

Costanza nodded, her brow furrowed. "And do you think he can succeed?"

Guido hesitated, then nodded slowly. "If anyone can, it's Grandfather. But this is no small undertaking. He must balance reform with tradition, appease the princes of Europe, and confront the Protestant leaders—all while holding the Church together."

"And if he fails?" she asked softly.

Guido's gaze darkened. "If he fails, the Church may never recover its unity. And the Farnese name, so closely tied to this endeavor, will bear the weight of that failure."

As letters from Rome began to arrive more frequently, Costanza followed the progress of the council with growing interest. The sessions, held in the northern Italian city of Trent, brought together bishops, cardinals, and theologians from across Europe. The issues at hand were monumental: the authority of the pope, the role of scripture and tradition, the sacraments, and the abuses that had fueled the Protestant Reformation.

One evening, a letter from her father detailed the early debates. *"The Council is divided,"* he wrote. *"Some seek to modernize the Church, to concede certain points to the Protestants. Others refuse to yield even an inch, fearing that any compromise will weaken the faith. I must navigate these waters carefully, for the wrong decision could fracture us further."*

Costanza shared the letter with her children, who read it with a frown. "Grandfather walks a narrow path," Mario said. "To reform without undermining the Church's authority—that is no easy feat."

As Costanza tended to her grandchildren and managed the affairs of Santa Fiora, her thoughts often drifted to Trent. She imagined her father seated among the greatest minds of the Church, his presence commanding and his voice a beacon of reason. She felt pride in his determination but also an undercurrent of fear. The Council of

Trent was not just a theological endeavor; it was a battleground for the soul of the Church.

~

Later that evening, Costanza took a quiet walk through the villa's gardens, her youngest grandchild cradled in her arms. The crisp winter air carried the scent of pine and earth, grounding her in the present even as her thoughts drifted to the uncertainty of the future. She found herself by Bosio's grave, a familiar haven shaded by tall olive trees. Kneeling by the carved stone marker, she placed a hand gently on its cool surface, her voice soft yet firm.

"This council," she murmured, her words mingling with the stillness of the evening, "It's about more than the Church. It's about our family. If Father succeeds, the Farnese name will be immortalized. If he fails…" She hesitated, the weight of the possibilities pressing against her chest.

The olive branches swayed in the breeze, their movement a silent witness to her reflection. She closed her eyes, her fingers brushing the stone as though seeking comfort in the memory of her husband. "You would tell me to trust him," she whispered. "To believe in his strength and vision, even when the path seems perilous. And you'd be right. You always were."

A faint smile touched her lips as she rose, brushing one hand on her gown. "I will honor your faith in me, Bosio. And I will honor his vision—for our children and grandchildren, for our name, and for the legacy you always believed in."

The distant toll of the chapel bell broke the stillness, its echo resonating through the hills of Santa Fiora. Costanza turned toward the villa, her resolve steeling. Whatever the outcome of her father's efforts, she would face it as she always had—with strength, grace, and an unshakable loyalty to the Farnese legacy.

~

In the months that followed, the council addressed pressing issues with a fervor that mirrored the urgency of the times. It reaffirmed key Catholic doctrines, including the authority of the pope and the importance of the sacraments, while enacting measures to address corruption within the clergy. The decisions made at Trent would shape the Counter-Reformation, strengthening the Church against the Protestant challenge.

For Costanza, the council became a symbol of her father's indomitable will—a reflection of the legacy he sought to leave for his family and the faith he served. As she read his letters, filled with updates on debates and resolutions, she felt a deep connection to the man who had always been both a towering figure and a loving father.

~

One evening, as she penned her response to his latest missive, she paused, the weight of her own words giving her pause. Finally, she wrote:

"Father, your work inspires us all. Though we are far from Trent, your family stands with you in spirit, and we are proud of all you have achieved. May God guide your hand and your heart, now and always."

As the ink dried, Costanza prayed for her father's success, knowing that the decisions made at Trent would ripple across generations. For the Church, for the Farnese family, and for the world, this was a moment that would endure in history—a testament to faith, resilience, and the power of vision.

Chapter 57

1545 a Farewell to Grace

The autumn wind swept through the hills of Santa Fiora, carrying with it the bittersweet scent of withering leaves and a hint of pine. Mario Sforza, now a young man of purpose and determination, stood outside the villa, staring at the distant horizon. The stillness of the air felt heavy, oppressive, as though the land itself sensed the gravity of the moment.

Inside, the household bustled quietly, the usual hum of life subdued. His mother, Costanza Farnese, had grown weaker with each passing day, the once-vibrant force of their family now confined to her bed. Mario had spent much of the day at her side, her voice soft but resolute as she shared her final words of wisdom.

"You are the strength of this family now," she had said, her hand cool against his. "Guide your siblings as Bosio would have. Carry our name with pride, but never let it blind you. Remember, Mario, legacy is built not by ambition alone but by the love and care we give to those who share it with us."

Those words played in his mind as he returned to her chamber later that evening. The flickering light of a single candle illuminated the room, casting shadows that danced like whispers against the walls. Costanza lay still, her face pale but serene, as though she had made peace with the inevitable.

He approached quietly, taking her hand in his. "Mother," he said, his voice trembling despite his effort to remain composed. "Is there anything more I can do for you?"

Her eyes, though dim with exhaustion, met his with unwavering clarity. "You have done everything already, Mario. You and your siblings are my greatest accomplishment. I leave this world knowing you will protect one another."

He swallowed the lump in his throat, nodding. "We will," he promised. "I will."

A faint smile curved her lips, and she exhaled slowly, her voice barely above a whisper. "Good. Then I can rest."

As the night wore on, Mario, as well as his siblings, remained by her side, the quiet of the room punctuated only by the rhythmic ticking of the clock and the faint sound of the wind outside. Just before dawn, she took one final, peaceful breath, and the weight of her passing settled over the villa like a shroud.

The family chapel, shaded by ancient olive trees, became the resting place for the matriarch who had guided them through so much. As the family gathered for her burial, Mario stood at the forefront, his young shoulders bearing the weight of their collective grief.

Guido's words echoed through the quiet air, a solemn reminder of the faith that had anchored Costanza throughout her life. Mario's siblings—Francesca, Giulia, and the younger children—stood beside him, their faces marked by sorrow and respect.

When it was his turn to speak, Mario stepped forward, his voice steady despite the emotion constricting his chest. "Our mother was more than the matriarch of this family. She was our heart, our guide, and our strength. Her legacy lives on in each of us, not just in name but in the values she instilled. We will honor her by carrying those values forward, by standing united as she taught us."

As they lowered her into the earth, Mario felt the weight of her absence settle over him. Yet, amidst the grief, there was a flicker of resolve—a determination to honor her memory, to lead as she had led, and to ensure that the Farnese and Sforza names endured with dignity and purpose.

In the days that followed, Mario often found himself drawn to his parent's graves. Beneath the towering olive trees, with the soft hum of the Tuscan breeze around him, he would sit in quiet contemplation.

"You told me to lead, Mother," he said one evening, his voice low but firm. "I will. But I wish you were here to guide me just a little longer."

The stars above seemed to twinkle in answer, a silent reassurance that her strength and wisdom would remain with him always. In that sacred space, Mario resolved to honor the promises he had made—to his mother, to his family, and to himself.

And as the first light of dawn broke over the hills, Mario rose, carrying forward the legacy of Costanza Farnese with the quiet grace she had embodied throughout her life.

Chapter 58

The summer sun of 1546 cast its golden light over the hills of Santa Fiora, but Mario Sforza's mind was far from the peaceful scenery of his home. Letters from Rome had arrived, bearing the seal of Pope Paul III, their contents as grand and ambitious as the man who had penned them. The legacy of his grandfather was growing with every passing year, leaving an indelible mark on Rome—and the Farnese name.

Mario sat in the study, the letter spread out before him. His youngest sister sat quietly nearby, her laughter a small comfort against the weight of the words he had just read.

"The Campidoglio," he murmured, running a hand through his hair. "Grandfather has Michelangelo redesigning Capitoline Hill. A trapezoidal piazza, they call it. And the Farnese

Palace—it's to have an Arch, connecting it to the Villa Farnesina."

His younger brother, Paulo, paused in the doorway, his brow furrowed with curiosity. "What does it mean, Mario? Why does Grandfather put so much into these projects?"

"It's legacy," Mario replied, his tone heavy with understanding. "Rome isn't just a city to him. It's a canvas, and every building, every piazza, is a brushstroke. It's how he ensures the Farnese name will never be forgotten."

~

In Rome, Michelangelo stood in his workshop, surveying the sprawling sketches before him. The Capitoline Hill, once a symbol of Rome's ancient glory, was to be reimagined under his hand. The pope had tasked him with creating a piazza that would not only elevate the city but serve as a testament to the unity of Church and state.

In his mind's eye, Michelangelo saw the completed design—the harmonious trapezoidal piazza, framed by majestic buildings. The Marcus Aurelius equestrian statue stood at its heart, a symbol of civic virtue and imperial strength. Every angle, every line, would guide the viewer's gaze toward the center, drawing them into the grandeur of the space.

Yet the challenges ahead loomed large. The construction itself would take years, and the political tensions of the time were palpable. Michelangelo knew that his work was as much a tool of diplomacy as it was an artistic endeavor.

Meanwhile, the death of Antonio da Sangallo the Younger that year left the Farnese Palace incomplete. Pope Paul III wasted no time appointing Michelangelo to oversee its continuation. While reluctant at first, Michelangelo soon found inspiration in the project, reimagining its courtyard with his bold, architectural genius.

The Farnese Arch, the centerpiece of his vision, was a daring concept: a bridge-like structure that would connect the Farnese Palace to the Villa Farnesina across the Tiber River. Michelangelo envisioned the Arch as a literal and symbolic bridge of power, uniting the Church's spiritual authority with the Farnese family's secular influence.

~

One quiet evening, Mario and his siblings gathered in the villa's garden, the letter from Rome spread out before them. The setting sun bathed the hills in amber hues, a stark contrast to the monumental projects described in their grandfather's words.

"The Arch is bold," Paulo said, his voice tinged with awe. "Connecting two palaces across the Tiber? It's like something out of legend."

"But also dangerous," Faustina interjected. "Grandfather's ambitions grow with every year. Not everyone will look kindly on such overt displays of power."

Mario nodded thoughtfully. "True. But these projects aren't just for the Farnese family. They're for Rome, for the Church. Grandfather believes in the eternal city, in its role as the heart of Christendom. Michelangelo's work is a reflection of that belief."

~

In Rome, Michelangelo oversaw the construction of the Campidoglio and the Farnese Palace, each stone placed with precision and purpose. For Pope Paul III, these projects were more than architectural marvels—they were declarations of faith, power, and legacy.

~

In Santa Fiora, Mario often visited the family chapel, where his mother, Costanza, now rested. As he knelt by her grave one evening, the weight of his family's legacy pressed heavily upon him.

"Mother," he whispered, his voice steady but soft. "I wonder what you would think of all this—Grandfather's plans, Michelangelo's genius, the Arch that will connect our name to the heart of Rome. You always believed in him, even when the stakes were high. I hope I can do the same."

The wind rustled the olive trees, carrying with it the faint scent of thyme and earth. Mario stood, his resolve firm. The Farnese name was both a blessing and a burden, but it was one he would carry, just as his mother had before him.

As the Campidoglio and Farnese Palace rose in grandeur, Michelangelo's vision began to take shape. For Mario, the letters from Rome were reminders of his family's place in history. His grandfather, Pope Paul III, was immortalizing their name through faith, art, and ambition.

But Mario also knew that such power came at a price. As he watched the first light of dawn crest the hills of Santa Fiora, he resolved to honor both his family's legacy and the quiet strength his mother had instilled in him.

For the Farnese name, for Rome, and for the enduring vision of Pope Paul III, he would stand as his family's anchor amidst the ever-shifting tides of power and ambition.

Chapter 59

The news arrived in Santa Fiora with the weight of a storm. Guido Sforza, now a young cardinal, returned home from Rome bearing a sealed letter marked with the crest of Pope Paul III. His journey had been swift and relentless, the urgency of his mission etched into his features as he entered the family villa.

Mario Sforza, standing in the central hall, turned at the sound of footsteps. His eyes met Guido's, and in that moment, he knew the news his brother carried was grave.

"Mario," Guido said, his voice steady but tinged with sorrow. He extended the letter, his fingers trembling ever so slightly. "This is from Grandfather."

Mario took the letter, breaking the seal with deliberate care. His eyes scanned the page, the weight of the words pressing down on him like a physical force.

"Pier Luigi is dead," he said finally, his voice low and controlled.

Across the room, their sister Faustina froze, her hands clutching the edge of a chair. "How?" she asked, her voice barely above a whisper.

Mario folded the letter, his jaw tightening as he faced them. "Assassinated. A conspiracy among the nobles of Piacenza. They struck while he was vulnerable, in his own fortress. The Emperor's forces nearby did nothing to stop it."

The siblings gathered in the villa's library, the gravity of the news settling over them like a heavy fog. Guido sat beside Faustina, his clerical robes a stark reminder of the family's ties to the Church. He had been present in Rome when the news reached Pope Paul III, and he recounted the pope's reaction with somber detail.

"Grandfather was devastated," Guido said. "Pier Luigi was his favorite. His death is not only a personal loss but a political one. The enemies who orchestrated this will not stop here."

Faustina, her hands folded tightly in her lap, looked at Mario. "What do we do now?"

Mario's expression was resolute. "We honor him by ensuring his death is not in vain. Grandfather has already moved to secure the Duchy for Ottavio. The Farnese name will endure, but we must remain vigilant."

That evening, Mario walked to the family burial site near the chapel, a familiar place of solace. The olive trees swayed gently in the evening breeze, their shadows long and somber against the fading light. He knelt beside Bosio's grave, the stone marker weathered but steadfast.

"Father," he murmured, his hand resting on the cool stone. "Pier Luigi is gone. His ambition, his fire—it's all been extinguished by those who envied his rise. But I will not let their betrayal define our family."

The wind carried the faint scent of wild thyme and earth, grounding him in the land they had called home for generations. Mario closed his eyes. The weight of leadership was heavy on his shoulders but familiar now. He thought of his siblings—Guido, with his quiet strength, and Faustina, with her perceptive mind—and knew that together, they could uphold the legacy their family had built.

The next morning, Mario and Guido stood together in the villa's gardens. Guido, though steeped in the politics of Rome, looked to his brother for guidance in navigating the uncertainty ahead.

"Grandfather will consolidate the Duchy," Guido said, breaking the silence. "But the nobles who betrayed Pier Luigi will not stop here. They see our family as a threat."

Mario nodded, his gaze fixed on the rolling hills of Santa Fiora. "Let them see us as a threat. It means we're doing something right. But we must be cautious. Ambition has claimed one of us already—we can't afford to lose more."

Faustina joined them, her presence quiet but steady. "Pier Luigi lived boldly," she said, her voice measured. "But boldness invites enemies. Perhaps we must learn to move with more subtlety."

Mario turned to her, a faint smile breaking through his solemn expression. "You've always been the wise one, Faustina. And you're right. The Farnese name will endure, but it must do so with both strength and strategy."

As the sun rose higher in the sky, casting its golden light over the villa, the siblings stood united in their resolve. Their uncle Pier Luigi's death was a tragedy, but it was also a reminder of the fragility of power. Together, they vowed to protect their family's legacy—not through reckless ambition, but through wisdom and unity.

Chapter 60

The sun filtered through the immense scaffolding surrounding St. Peter's Basilica, casting long shadows on the half-finished walls and domes that had stood in limbo for decades. Michelangelo Buonarroti, now in his seventies, walked slowly through the construction site, his sharp eyes scanning every detail. Though his body bore the weight of age, his mind was as sharp as the tools he had once wielded as a young sculptor.

For years, St. Peter's Basilica had been a patchwork of visions, each architect leaving their mark but none bringing the project to completion. Antonio da Sangallo the Younger's recent death had left a void, and now, under the direction of Pope Paul III, the task had fallen squarely to Michelangelo.

The Apostolic Palace bustled with activity as Michelangelo prepared to present his revised plans to Pope Paul III. Francesca, accompanying her Grandfather on a rare visit to the basilica, watched from a discreet corner of the room. She had grown accustomed to her grandfather's discussions with artists and architects, but Michelangelo's presence had a different gravity.

The pope, seated in a grand chair, leaned forward as Michelangelo unrolled the parchment, revealing the sweeping vision of a centralized, Greek-cross layout.

"Magnificent," Pope Paul III murmured, his fingers tracing the lines of the dome. "You've captured the divine in stone, Michelangelo."

The artist, known for his brusque demeanor, offered a small nod. "The center of the Church must reflect the heavens themselves—perfect, balanced, eternal."

Francesca observed Michelangelo's design with a mix of wonder and curiosity. She had heard her Grandfather speak of the dome as a symbol of the Church's power and its unity, but seeing it take shape in Michelangelo's plans brought those words to life.

"It's breathtaking," she whispered to her Grandfather. "A testament not just to God, but to human ambition."

The pope's gaze softened as he looked at her. "And a legacy, Francesca. One that will outlast all of us."

~

Days turned into weeks as Michelangelo immersed himself in the task of transforming St. Peter's Basilica. He dismantled much of Sangallo's work, stripping away unnecessary embellishments to focus on clarity and grandeur. His vision centered on the dome—a monumental structure that would dominate Rome's skyline and symbolize the Church's connection to the divine.

Michelangelo's passion was evident in every detail. He reworked the interior spaces to harmonize with the central dome, creating a sense of balance and symmetry that elevated the soul. The columns, the arches, the very stones seemed to echo his dedication to both art and faith.

One afternoon, Francesca found herself standing at the edge of the construction site, watching the workers haul massive blocks of stone. Michelangelo stood nearby, his expression a mix of frustration and focus as he directed the masons.

"You seem troubled, Master Michelangelo," she said, stepping closer.

He turned, his face softening slightly at her presence. "Troubled? Always. There's no art without struggle, my lady."

Francesca smiled faintly. "My Grandfather speaks highly of you and your work here. He says it will be your greatest masterpiece."

Michelangelo's gaze drifted to the unfinished dome. "It is not my masterpiece, but God's. I am merely the hand that shapes the stone."

She studied him for a moment, struck by the humility in his words. "Do you ever doubt?" she asked. "That the vision in your mind can be realized?"

He chuckled, the sound low and dry. "Every day, my lady. But doubt is the fire that forges resolve. Without it, we are complacent. And complacency is the death of creation."

As the dome began to take shape, the scale of Michelangelo's work became evident. Visitors from across Europe came to marvel at the construction, their awe a testament to the artist's vision.

For Francesca, the basilica became a symbol of her Grandfather's papacy—a tangible expression of the Farnese legacy. She often returned to the site, her own children in tow, to watch the progress. Standing beneath the rising dome, she felt both small and significant, a part of something far greater than herself.

In the quiet of the Farnese Palace, Francesca spoke with her brothers about the grandeur of St. Peter's and Michelangelo's relentless pursuit of perfection.

"He seems possessed by it," she said. "As though the basilica is more than a building—it's a testament to his faith and his fears."

Paulo nodded thoughtfully. "Great men are often driven by more than ambition. Perhaps Michelangelo sees this as his way of leaving a mark on eternity."

"And our Grandfather?" Francesca asked. "What does he see?"

"A legacy," Paulo replied simply. "One that will endure long after we are gone."

As the months turned into years, Michelangelo's work on St. Peter's Basilica progressed, though he knew he might never see it completed in his lifetime. Yet his vision endured, carried forward by those who followed, and Francesca, like the rest of the world, bore witness to a creation that transcended its time—a beacon of faith, art, and ambition.

Chapter 61

The late spring air of 1548 carried a sense of anticipation to the Sforza villa in Santa Fiora. Mario Sforza stood in the villa's courtyard, his mind preoccupied with the burdens left to him in the wake of his mother and father's deaths. The sound of hooves approached, and he turned to see his older brother, Guido, dismounting his horse with practiced ease. In Guido's hand was a letter sealed with the unmistakable crest of Pope Paul III.

"From Grandfather," Guido said, handing the letter to Mario. His expression, usually composed, held a trace of concern.

Mario took the letter, broke the seal and scanned the contents. His jaw tightened as he read, each word carrying the weight of their family's future. He looked up at Guido, his voice steady but tinged with unease. "Ottavio has been officially installed as the Duke of Parma and Piacenza. Grandfather has secured the title, but Charles V will not take this lightly."

Nearby, their sister Faustina approached, her brow furrowed. "What does it mean for us?" she asked.

Mario handed her the letter, his gaze fixed on the horizon. "It means Ottavio must prove himself. The Duchy is a prize, but it comes with enemies—both within and without."

The news of Ottavio's ascension spread quickly, bringing with it both congratulations and veiled threats. Letters from Rome detailed the strained relationship between the young duke and Emperor Charles V. The emperor, wary of the Farnese family's growing power, viewed Ottavio's installation as a direct challenge to his authority.

That evening, Mario joined Guido, Faustina, and Paulo for dinner in the villa's grand hall. The atmosphere was heavy, the weight of the news palpable.

"Grandfather has done what he always does," Guido said, his tone measured. "He's secured the family's position. But our cousin Ottavio is young, and the emperor will test him."

Faustina set down her goblet, her expression thoughtful. "Youth can be a strength or a weakness, depending on how it's wielded. Do you think Ottavio is ready for this?"

Mario leaned back in his chair, his fingers drumming lightly on the table. "He has no choice but to be ready. Grandfather has placed him in a position of immense power, and with that comes immense risk. But Ottavio carries the Farnese name, and that name demands resilience."

~

Weeks later, a Jesuit priest arrived at the villa, bringing news of the Church's ongoing reforms and the growing influence of the Society of Jesus. Father Matteo, a soft-spoken man with keen eyes, joined the siblings for a modest meal.

"The Holy Father has guided the Jesuits well," Father Matteo said, his voice calm. "Their mission expands daily, strengthening the Church's foundation."

Mario nodded thoughtfully. "But at what cost? The Jesuits inspire loyalty, yes, but they also draw scrutiny. And the Inquisition—how does that play into this strategy?"

Father Matteo's expression darkened. "The Roman Inquisition is a necessary response to the threats of heresy. It is not a path chosen lightly, but it is one the Church must walk."

Guido, ever the diplomat, added, "The Inquisition is a tool, one that must be wielded with precision. Grandfather knows this better than anyone."

~

Later that summer, Mario and Guido traveled to Rome to visit the Farnese Palace. The city was alive with the hum of activity, its streets bustling with merchants, nobles, and clergy. The palace itself was a testament to the family's ambition, its grandeur enhanced by Michelangelo's ongoing work on the Farnese Arch.

In the pope's private chambers, Mario and Guido were greeted by their grandfather, who, despite his age, exuded an aura of authority.

"Mario, Guido," Pope Paul III said, his voice warm but firm. "The Farnese name has faced many challenges, but we endure. Ottavio's position is secure—for now. But he must navigate carefully. The emperor's eyes are on him."

"And Charles V?" Mario asked, his tone cautious.

The pope's expression hardened. "He is displeased, as expected. But the Duchy is ours. Ottavio must prove himself worthy of it. That is his burden to bear."

~

Back in Santa Fiora, Mario walked through the villa's gardens with Faustina, the evening air cool and fragrant with wild thyme. The weight of the family's legacy pressed heavily on his shoulders, but he bore it with the quiet strength his mother had taught him.

"Do you think Ottavio can handle this?" Faustina asked, breaking the silence.

Mario paused, his gaze fixed on the distant hills. "He is young, but he is a Farnese. He will learn, as we all have, that resilience is not a choice—it is a necessity."

Faustina nodded, her expression pensive. "And Grandfather? How long can he hold everything together?"

"As long as he must," Mario said. "He's built this legacy with his own hands, but it's up to us to uphold it. For Ottavio, for the Farnese name, for all of us."

As the sun dipped below the horizon, Mario resolved to support his family in whatever way he could. The Farnese name carried power, but it also carried immense responsibility. Together, they would navigate the challenges ahead, their legacy shaped by resilience, ambition, and the enduring strength of their bond.

Chapter 62

The winter of 1549 settled heavily over Rome, its cold air carrying an unfamiliar stillness. The Vatican's grand halls, usually alive with activity and the murmur of political intrigue, had grown somber. Pope Paul III, the towering figure of reform and ambition, now lay confined to his bed in the Apostolic Palace. The years of leadership, marked by the grandeur of the Counter-Reformation and the weight of familial legacy, had taken their toll.

Mario Sforza arrived in Rome at the summons of his cousin, Cardinal Alessandro Farnese the Younger. The journey from Santa Fiora had been solemn, the weight of his family's legacy pressing upon him. Now, standing within the austere walls of the Vatican, Mario could feel the gravity of the moment—the end of an era drawing near.

The pope's private chamber was dimly lit, the flickering light of candles casting long shadows on the ornate walls. Alessandro Farnese the Younger, now a cardinal of considerable influence, stood at the foot of the pope's bed, his expression composed but deeply affected.

"Mario," Cardinal Alessandro said softly, turning to him. "Come closer. He's been asking for you."

Mario approached the frail figure of his grandfather. Pope Paul III lay propped against silken pillows, his face pale and gaunt, yet his eyes retained a sharpness that defied his declining body.

"Mario," the pope murmured, his voice weak but resolute.

Mario knelt beside the bed, his heart heavy. "Holy Father," he said reverently, his voice thick with emotion.

The pope's lips curved faintly. "You carry the Sforza name, but you are Farnese in spirit. Stand, my boy. Let me see the man you've become."

Rising, Mario clasped his grandfather's frail hand in his own. "You have guided us all, Grandfather. Your strength has been our foundation."

The pope's gaze softened. "Strength... it has always been a burden as much as a gift. My son, you must carry it now. For your family, for your name."

For weeks, the Farnese family had been summoned to Rome. Cardinal Alessandro oversaw the household's organization and tended to the pope's spiritual needs, while Mario found himself navigating the delicate balance of grief and duty.

When the news came that Pope Paul III's health had taken a dire turn, the family gathered in his private chapel. Cardinals, clerics, and trusted advisors surrounded him for what would be his final mass.

Mario stood alongside Faustina, his younger sister, whose quiet strength mirrored that of their late mother, Costanza. Together, they watched as Cardinal Alessandro led the prayers, his voice steady but breaking at moments under the weight of the occasion. The chapel, illuminated by the flickering glow of candlelight, seemed to hold its breath as the prayers echoed through its vaulted ceilings.

Mario glanced at his grandfather, whose frail form seemed almost swallowed by the grandeur of the setting. Yet, even in his final moments, Pope Paul III radiated an unyielding presence. It was as if the man who had shaped the Counter-Reformation, secured the Farnese legacy, and reshaped the Church still held the weight of the world upon his shoulders.

After the mass, Alessandro Farnese the Younger approached the pontiff's bedside, his composure unwavering. One by one, the family members drew near, kneeling to receive the pope's blessing.

Mario knelt first, his heart pounding. "Mario," the pope said, his voice barely a whisper. "Though you are a Sforza, you carry the Farnese blood. Honor it, protect it, and never forget the weight it bears."

"I won't, Grandfather," Mario vowed, his voice resolute despite the lump in his throat.

Faustina approached next, her soft footsteps echoing in the silent chamber. Alessandro's gaze lingered on her, his expression tender. "My dear Faustina," he murmured, "You remind me so much of your mother. Be her strength, as she was mine."

Tears welled in Faustina's eyes as she nodded. "I will, Holy Father."

Cardinal Alessandro was last. Kneeling before his grandfather, his voice faltered as he said, "Holy Father, your legacy will guide us all."

Alessandro raised a trembling hand, tracing a final blessing over his grandson's head. "You are the light of this family, Alessandro. Lead them well."

As the family stepped back, Alessandro Farnese—the pope and patriarch—took his last breath. Silence filled the room, broken only by the solemn tolling of bells outside, announcing the passing of one of the Church's greatest reformers.

Mario stood by the window, staring out at the first light of dawn breaking over Rome. The bells of St. Peter's Basilica tolled, their mournful tones echoing through the city.

He turned back to the room, his gaze falling on his grandfather's still form. "The world will remember him as a reformer, a statesman, and a pope," he said softly to Cardinal Alessandro, his cousins, and his siblings. "But to us, he was a father, a grandfather—a man who gave everything for his family and his Church."

Faustina, her face streaked with tears, took Mario's hand. "And now it is up to us to carry forward his legacy."

Cardinal Alessandro placed a hand on Mario's shoulder, his expression solemn. "The Farnese name has always carried weight. But together, we will carry it forward."

Stepping into the brisk morning air, Mario whispered a silent prayer. "We will honor you, Grandfather. We will make you proud."

Chapter 63

The morning light of Rome in the 1560s streamed through the towering windows of St. Peter's Basilica, casting a golden glow upon the monument of Pope Paul III. Mario Sforza stood before his grandfather's tomb, his chest tightening with a mix of pride and reverence. The towering effigy, sculpted with lifelike precision by Guglielmo della Porta, reflected the serene dignity his grandfather had carried throughout his papacy. Beneath the effigy, the allegories of Prudence and Justice stood as eternal witnesses to the virtues that defined his reign.

Mario's fingers brushed the cold marble of the tomb as if seeking some connection to the man who had shaped their family's destiny. His thoughts drifted to the countless stories told within their family, the victories, the sacrifices, the unrelenting ambition of Pope Paul III.

"Grandfather," he whispered, his voice steady despite the emotion swelling in his chest, "We stand because of you. The Farnese name flourishes because of the path you forged."

As Mario knelt before the monument, his mind filled with the lessons his grandfather had imparted. Paul III had been more than a pope or a patriarch; he was the architect of a legacy that transcended marble and stone.

Rising, Mario turned his gaze to the grand dome above, its vastness reminding him of the enduring spirit of the Church and the Farnese name. Though the weight of their family's history pressed upon him, it also lifted him, guiding him forward.

~

Rome 1981 - 2024

Centuries later, the grandeur of St. Peter's Basilica never fails to command awe. Its towering dome, shimmering mosaics, and intricate sculptures are a testament to centuries of faith and ambition. My first visit to this sacred space was at the age of fifteen, wide-eyed and overwhelmed by its sheer scale. It left an impression—a sense of wonder—but at that time, I was merely a tourist, unaware of the deeper connections I would later uncover.

At nineteen, I returned to Rome, eager to revisit the Vatican. This time, I stepped inside St. Peter's Basilica, its magnificence drawing me in like a magnet. The grandeur of the space, the whispers of history, and the reverence that filled the air all lingered in my memory. Yet, it wasn't until many years later that I understood the significance of what I had seen.

At twenty-one, I tried to visit the basilica again, but fate kept me at a distance. The Vatican seemed out of reach, as though it was waiting for the right moment to reveal its secrets. That moment came in October 2024, when I walked through the vast halls of the basilica with a sense of purpose, no longer just a visitor but a seeker retracing a story that had shaped both history and my own understanding of legacy.

When I stood before the same tomb in 2024, it was as though my ancestor's voice echoed faintly in the air. The marble effigy seemed to hold the weight of centuries, yet it carried a sense of timelessness. As I viewed the lines of the allegorical statues, I thought of my grandfather's name, *Alessandro Farnese, His Holiness Pope Paul III, Bishop of Rome, Vicar of Jesus Christ, Successor of Saint Peter, Supreme Pontiff of the Universal Church, Primate of Italy, Archbishop and Metropolitan of the Roman Province, Sovereign of the Vatican City State, and Servant of the Servants of God.*

I reached out, my fingers brushing the cold stone of the main alter, just a few feet away from him, and in that moment, the past felt vividly alive. It wasn't just a tomb I stood before—it was a bridge between generations. Mario had seen this place through the lens of personal loss, and now, centuries later, I saw it as a writer piecing together fragments of my own family's story. It was a story that belonged not just to the Farnese family, but to anyone who carries the weight of legacy.

I raised my camera, framing the monument as the light caught its intricate details. Each click was a silent prayer, a promise to carry this story forward.

From Mario's time to mine, the tomb of Pope Paul III has stood as a testament to ambition, faith, and the sacrifices made in pursuit of a vision. For Mario, it was deeply personal—a place to connect with the man who had shaped his family and the Church. For me, it was a moment of understanding, a realization that legacies endure not just in marble and stone but in the lives they touch.

As I turned to leave the basilica that day, I whispered a reflection to myself, words that seemed to echo Mario's sentiment across time: "We carry them with us. In our words, in our memories, in the places they've touched. We carry them, and we honor them."

The soft light of St. Peter's filtered through the towering arches, casting gentle beams across the nave. As I walked beside my husband, a quiet sense of reverence settled over me. The story of Pope Paul III, of Costanza, of Mario, and even my own journey was not confined to the pages of history. It lived on—in the hearts of those who remember, in the stories we pass down, and in the legacies we choose to honor and preserve.

Lineage

Alessandro Farnèse (Pope Paul III) 1468 -
1549 and his mistress **Silvia Ruffini** 1475 -
1561. Their children:

- Costanza Farnèse (my grandaunt)
  1500–1545
- **Pier Luigi Alexander Farnèse**
  (Hertog van Parma) II (my
  grandfather) 1503–1547
- Paolo Farnese (my granduncle) 1504–
  1513
- Ranuccio Farnese (my granduncle)
  1509–1529

Pier Luigi Alexander Farnèse's daughter, **Vittoria Farnese** Duchessa di Urbino 1521–1602. Her daughter, **Lavinia Feltria della Rovere**, Princess of Francavilla 1558 – 1632. Her daughter, Princess **Isabela D'avalos D'aquino D'aragona** IX marquesa de Pescara 1585 - 1648. Her daughter, **Jeanne Nicole d'Aragon** 1602 – 1657. Her son, **François Gariépy** 1629 – 1706. His son, **Francois Gariepy Jr.** 1665 – 1738. His son, **Charles Gariepy** 1691 – 1752. His son, **Louis-Joseph Gariépy** 1729 – 1782. His son, **Joseph Gariépy** 1765 – 1836. His son, **Olivier Gariépy** 1800 – 1849. His son, **Oliver Alfred Edmond Gariépy** 1827 – 1908. His daughter, **Marie Louise Julie Gariépy** 1856 – 1921,. Her daughter, **Marie Eliza Juliette Desjardins** 1896 – 1978. Her son, **Jean Paul Pilon** 1923 – 1989. His daughter, **Mary Linda Juliette Pilon** 1949 at the time of this writing – Living. Her daughter, **Connie Anne Lenora Fletcher** *(Constance Santego)* 1966 at the time of this writing – Living.

A Prayer for Strength and Grace

Heavenly Father,

In the shadows of doubt and the weight of legacy, grant me the strength to walk my path with courage. Teach me to embrace my imperfections, for it is through them that Your grace shines most brightly.

Guide my heart to forgive the past and to honor the truth within my soul. May I find wisdom in every challenge, humility in every triumph, and peace in every storm.

Help me to weave my story with love and purpose, knowing that even in the broken threads, Your design is perfect.

Through Your infinite mercy, may I rise above judgment and fear, and live as a reflection of Your light, ever faithful to Your will.

Amen.

Acknowledgments

Writing *Illegitimate Grace* has been a journey of discovery, inspiration, and immense gratitude. This novel would not have come to life without the contributions, encouragement, and support of many.

First and foremost, I would like to thank the scholars, historians, and archivists who have dedicated themselves to preserving the fascinating details of Renaissance Italy and the lives entwined within it. Their meticulous work provided the foundation for this fictional exploration of Costanza Farnese's story.

To my family, thank you for your endless patience, love, and belief in this project. Your support gave me the strength to dive into the past and unearth the narrative waiting to be told.

A heartfelt thanks to my mentors, colleagues, and fellow writers who offered insights, feedback, and encouragement. Your wisdom and constructive criticism guided me through the intricate weaving of fact and fiction.

To my readers, thank you for taking the time to step into Costanza's world. My hope is that this story not only entertains but also provides a new perspective on the resilience, strength, and complexity of those who shaped history in ways both seen and unseen.

Finally, I extend my gratitude to the creative spirit that whispered this tale into being. The process of writing *Illegitimate Grace* has been one of profound connection—to history, to imagination, and to the timeless truths of the human experience.

With deepest thanks,
Dr. Constance Santego

Footnotes & Bibliography

This novel, while a work of fiction, draws upon historical events, figures, and cultural practices of Renaissance Italy for its setting and inspiration. Every effort has been made to capture the essence of the time, though creative liberties have been taken to weave a compelling narrative.

The following sources and references provided invaluable context and insight into the world of the Farnese family and the broader Renaissance period. These works helped shape the historical backdrop against which the story unfolds:

Bibliography

1. **Williams, George L.** *Papal Genealogy: The Families and Descendants of the Popes.* McFarland & Company, 2004.
2. **McIver, Katherine A.** *Wives, Widows, Mistresses, and Nuns in Early Modern Italy: Making the Invisible Visible through Art and Patronage.* Ashgate, 2012.

3. **Hibbert, Christopher.** *The Borgias and Their Enemies: 1431-1519.* Houghton Mifflin Harcourt, 2008.
4. **Rowland, Ingrid D.** *The Culture of the High Renaissance: Ancients and Moderns in Sixteenth-Century Rome.* Cambridge University Press, 1998.
5. **Burke, Peter.** *The Italian Renaissance: Culture and Society in Italy.* Polity Press, 1986.

Additional References

- Archival documents and genealogical records concerning the Farnese family, sourced through public databases and historical compilations.
- Insights from art and architecture of Renaissance Rome, including works by Gian Lorenzo Bernini and Guglielmo della Porta, which influenced descriptions in the novel.

Acknowledgment of Creative License

While these sources inspired the novel, many characters, events, and details are products of the author's imagination. They have been shaped to enhance the narrative and explore the themes of identity, legacy, and resilience. Readers are encouraged to explore the referenced works for a deeper understanding of the historical context.

The Author

Constance Santego *Ph.D., DNM*

Dr. Constance Santego is an accomplished author, educator, and holistic healer whose passion for history, spirituality, and personal transformation has inspired readers around the globe. With a doctoral degree in Natural Medicine and decades of experience in the healing arts, Constance brings a unique perspective to her storytelling, seamlessly blending historical depth with timeless themes of resilience, identity, and empowerment.

Growing up in a town rich with folklore and natural beauty, Constance developed an early fascination with the intersection of history, myth, and human experience. Her journey of exploration has taken her to places as diverse as Italy, Greece, Spain, and England, where she delved into the art, culture, and stories that shaped the world.

As a writer, Constance combines her academic background with her love for narrative fiction to create works that are both thought-provoking and deeply engaging. Her novels often explore the lives of historical figures, reimagining their worlds through vivid detail and emotional depth. With *Illegitimate Grace*, she invites readers into the Renaissance courts of Rome, where power, legacy, and personal strength collide in a tale inspired by the life of Costanza Farnese, the illegitimate daughter of Pope Paul III.

Constance's dedication to holistic healing and personal development continues to influence her literary works, offering readers not just a story but an opportunity for reflection and growth. Her novels inspire readers to look beyond the surface, uncovering the universal truths hidden within history's most compelling narratives.

When she's not writing, Constance enjoys life in a serene lakeside community, surrounded by family, nature, and the quiet inspiration that fuels her creativity. Her mission remains steadfast: to guide others toward healing, understanding, and a deeper connection with the past and the present.

St. Peter's Basilica

Monument to Pope Paul III. This funerary monument, crafted by sculptor Guglielmo della Porta, is located to the left of the Altar of the Chair within the Basilica.

**An Artistic Interpretation of Pope Paul III
and His Daughter, Costanza Farnese.**

9 781990 062513